CHASING DANGER

MYSTERY AT THE ICE HOTEL

Scholastic Children's Books
An imprint of Scholastic Ltd
Euston House, 24 Eversholt Street, London, NW1 1DB, UK
Registered office: Westfield Road, Southam, Warwickshire, CV47 0RA

First published in the UK by Scholastic Ltd, 2016

ISBN 978 1407 16330 7

A CIP catalogue record for this book
is available from the British Library.

Printed by CPI Group (UK) Ltd, Croydon, CR0 4YY
Papers used by Scholastic Children's Books are made
from wood grown in sustainable forests.

1 3 5 7 9 10 8 6 4 2

www.scholastic.co.uk

CHASING DANGER

MYSTERY AT THE ICE HOTEL

SARA GRANT

SCHOLASTIC

TO THE EXTRAORDINARY LIBRARIANS, TEACHERS, FACULTY AND STUDENTS OF THE BROXBOURNE SCHOOL. IT'S A PLEASURE TO BE YOUR PATRON OF READING. KEEP READING AND WRITING!

AND

TO JESSICA WEBSTER FOR WINNING BROXBOURNE'S FIRST CREATIVE WRITING COMPETITION. CHECK OUT HER STORY AT THE BACK OF THE BOOK!

1

I slammed my back against the tree trunk and locked eyes with Mackenzie. She was crouched behind another tree a few feet away. Our breath puffed little clouds in the icy air. I slowly scanned our surroundings. No sign of them anywhere, but they were out there, waiting to attack.

Snowflakes fluttered down, blanketing the forest in silence. We had tracked them here, but they had zigzagged in the snow to mask their exact hiding spot.

What was that?

My body stiffened. The sound was no louder than the flutter of wings. Or was that the crunch of snow under tiptoe?

There it was again. Mackenzie'd heard it too.

We were sitting ducks if we stayed here. They were better trackers. They'd lived in this forest all their lives, running every inch of it. What chance did we have to outsmart them? But we had to try.

I gestured to Mackenzie that it was time to move. She nodded. My gloved hand counted down.

Three . . . two . . . one. . .

We bolted from hiding, lunging forward from tree to tree. The snow was more than a foot deep, and we struggled to move in our snowsuits and boots. The protective gear and our heavy breathing deadened our senses. We didn't hear them coming.

"AAAHHH!" Mackenzie screamed as Killer pounced on her from behind.

I whipped around in time to see Rocky spring from his hiding place and shove me to the ground. His paws pinned my shoulders. His piercing blue eyes studied me. I knew what was coming. I closed my eyes and buried my face in the hood of my snowsuit.

His slobbery tongue licked my cheek. *Yuk!* I wrapped my arms around his fluffy black fur and tumbled in the snow with him. "You caught me," I said, and scratched him behind the ears.

Mackenzie was giggling and wriggling in the snow, failing to fend off Killer's doggy kisses.

"Chase! Mackenzie!" My grandma was calling us. "Mackenzie! Chase!" Her voice twisted among the trees.

The huskies froze. Their ears pricked up. I leaped to my feet and tried to determine where the sound had come from. After our game of hide 'n' seek with the dogs, I was a bit lost.

"A little help?" Mackenzie asked as she flailed in the snow. They didn't have model-sized gear here. The smallest snowsuit was still a size too big for Mackenzie. She'd belted it at the waist. Only she could make bulky snow gear look Paris–catwalk awesome.

I checked the new chunky, silver sports watch Grandma had given me. Actually she'd given Mackenzie and me complete new winter wardrobes because we'd lost everything when pirates had attacked our island in the Maldives. That seemed a lifetime ago, even though only two weeks had passed.

This weekend Grandma would launch her new business – a dating app for singles over sixty-five years old – at a resort inside the Arctic Circle in Sweden. And her first guests were about to arrive.

I helped Mackenzie up and asked, "Which way?" I could almost see her computer-like brain whirring.

"This way." She pointed to the right.

"Killer! Rocky!" Robert, the lead musher, shouted. The dogs dashed in the direction Mackenzie was pointing.

"Come on," I said, and tore off after them.

Within seconds the huskies had raced out of sight. We followed their tracks to a small airport as a private jet landed on the almost entirely snow-covered runway.

"There you are," Grandma said, and waved us over to the airplane hangar. She hugged us close. "Remember our cover story?" she whispered. Mackenzie and I nodded. After someone had tried to kill Mackenzie in the Maldives, we made sure everyone believed that the bad guys had succeeded. Mackenzie Clifford was presumed dead. It was the only way to keep her safe. "You are my two granddaughters; you're cousins," she reminded us.

I stared at Mackenzie, finding it difficult to believe that anyone could think we were related, but so far no one had questioned it. We were both fourteen, but other than our age, we were complete opposites. She was black. I was white. She was raised in London. I grew up on a farm in Indiana. She was tall and thin. I was short and athletic. She was a computer genius and had created Grandma's new app. I was better at anything sporty. She looked ready for a photo shoot with always-glossed lips, painted nails and perfect red-brown spiral curls that created this hair halo. I was ready for action. My wardrobe usually consisted of T-shirts from fun runs and bike races. My long blonde hair was always tied back. If we were family, she had inherited most of the good genes, and I made do with the leftovers.

"When you were shouting for us, you called her Mackenzie," I corrected Grandma.

Grandma shook her head in frustration. "What am I supposed to call her?"

"Berkeley," Mackenzie and I said together.

"Berkeley, that's right." Grandma nodded. She wasn't usually so absent-minded, but I could tell she was worried about this weekend and her new business. "Remind me. Why Berkeley?"

Mackenzie got to pick the fake name that fit her new resurrected persona. "Berkeley was the name of a famous White Hat Hacker," she explained. "She blew the whistle on several really bad companies..." On and on she went about techo-gobbledygook.

"We get it already," I griped.

"Anyway, ladies," Grandma said to draw our attention back to the here and now. "How do I look?" Grandma combed her fingers through her short silvery hair. Everyone else wore the standard blue-and-black snowsuits issued by the Winter Wonder Resort, but Grandma's suit was bright red to match the Love Late in Life logo. She was pretty amazing for sixty-nine years old. "I'm going to greet our guests. You help Shauna. This is her first big event-planning job. I want everything to go well." She smoothed on red lipstick and pinched her already rosy cheeks. "And so it begins," she said, and walked towards the plane parking outside the hangar.

"Her first job?" I didn't know that.

"Shauna pursued Ariadne for months," Mackenzie whispered. "Ariadne didn't give her the job at first, but Shauna sent a huge binder with every detail of Ariadne's launch weekend planned, and Ariadne changed her mind. She loves someone with tenacity."

I'd have to remember that: Never take *no* for an answer. I liked Shauna even more for her tenacity.

Shauna rushed over. Like always she had her black messenger bag slung across her body and her clipboard in her hand. Shauna had to-do lists and timelines that mapped out every minute. You'd never guess that she was only nineteen.

"This is thrilling!" Shauna beamed. "Are we ready?" She looked from Mackenzie to me but didn't give us a chance to respond. "Of course we are! Team Love Late in Life! High five!" She raised her hand, and we didn't leave her hanging. "Let's go! Let's go! Let's go! I'm going to collect the luggage and drive it to the resort." It was weird how she sounded posh and British like the Queen even when she was talking fast like a sports commentator. "I'd be ever so grateful if you could check in our guests and show them to their assigned dogsleds." She handed the clipboard to me.

I batted it away. "Aren't these the VIPs?" I asked. "Are you sure you shouldn't check them in?"

"You can do it!" She clapped. For a second I thought she might break into a cheer. "We reviewed this at our pre-event meeting last night."

She cocked her head and smirked at me. We'd gone over the itinerary and what everyone was supposed to do and when they were supposed to do it, like, a million times. Mackenzie had memorized it so my only plan was to follow her. "Ariadne will greet the grandparents and you'll make the grandchildren feel welcome."

Shauna had suggested inviting single grandparents and one of their grandchildren. Grandma loved the idea of Mackenzie and me having kids our own age around. I thought it was a weird PR stunt, but Shauna said if the grandkids were happy then the grandparents would be too. The grandparents were potential investors and influential friends of friends. If the VIPs liked the app and had a good weekend then Love Late in Life would be a success. Tonight was the VIP party. Tomorrow the rest of the guests would arrive to launch the app with events and activities planned nearly every hour.

Mackenzie took the clipboard and ran her finger down the list of names. "I assume dogsled number one is up front with Rocky and Killer leading the pack. They are statistically the fastest. . ." Mackenzie and Shauna continued with their mind-melding geek speak.

"Here they come," I said as a mismatched grandmother and granddaughter marched towards us. The grandmother was tall and lanky with her hair pulled in a tight bun. The girl was all curves and long, wavy brown hair, which she flipped from side to side as she sauntered a few steps behind her grandma. From the photos Shauna had given us, I recognized retired headmistress Lucinda Sterling and her nineteen-year-old granddaughter Alexia.

"I'll see you back at the resort," Shauna blurted and hurried off. She suddenly seemed nervous. It was her first big gig. It must be like the jolt of panic I felt at the start of a race; even if I had trained, I was always mega jittery for the first few minutes.

"Hello, Mrs and Miss Sterling," I said, and tugged off my gloves. I extended my hand. Mrs Sterling shook it. Alexia slipped a mobile phone out of her tiny purple handbag that matched her ridiculously inappropriate heels and tapped on the screen. "I'm Chase and this is Berkeley. Welcome to the Arctic Circle and the launch of Love Late in Life. A weekend to melt hearts and make memories." I said the slogan just as we had practised with Shauna.

Alexia rolled her eyes.

"I love your Prada," Mackenzie said to Alexia. I assumed she meant the handbag and shoes. Mackenzie loved all that stuff. Alexia didn't even look up from her phone. Rude!

I consulted Mackenzie's clipboard. "You and Alexia are on the last dogsled. Bingo and Bongo are your lead dogs."

"I am not travelling by dog," Alexia said, still focused on her phone.

"It will be an experience," Mrs Sterling said, standing straight and tall like a soldier at attention.

"It will be cold," Alexia whined.

"There are loads of blankets on the sled," I informed them. "We have extra coats, hats and gloves, or we can give you your snowsuits now."

Alexia crinkled her nose as if she'd whiffed

something gross. "No, I don't think so."

"The ride will be scenic, my dear," Mrs Sterling said, her tone so flat that even I didn't think it sounded fun any more.

"It will be smelly," Alexia said, and crossed her arms high across her chest.

Mrs Sterling looped her arm around my shoulders as if we were old friends. She steered me a few feet away. "I'm sure you can find a nice car to take us to the resort," she told me. "We don't want to upset Alexia, do we, Charlie?"

Actually *we* don't care about your spoiled brat of a granddaughter. "I'm Chase," I corrected.

"Yes, yes, whatever." Mrs Sterling flapped her hands to shoo me away. "Run along and find us a car, will you?"

Ooooh, they were so annoying. My fingers curled into fists. I was about to tell the Sterlings what they could do with their special requests, when I spotted Grandma checking the dogsleds. *Grandma.* I still found it hard to believe that I had a real live grandma at last. I'd met her for the first time a few weeks ago. This weekend was super important to her. I didn't want to mess up with one of her very important guests.

"You and Alexia can ride in the SUV over there." I pointed to the vehicle and driver both sporting the resort logo. Shauna, Mackenzie and I were supposed to ride in SUVs so we would arrive at the resort before the guests on the sleds. Shauna must have already left. Mrs Sterling didn't even say *thank you* as she showed Alexia to the SUV.

When everyone had checked in and were snuggling on to their dogsleds, I explained to Grandma and Mackenzie what had happened.

"You can take their places on the last dogsled," Grandma said. "I'll lead the way with Robert, Killer and Rocky."

I gave an excited little jump and teeny, tiny professional *yippee!*

"Are you sure it's not too snowy for a dogsled ride?" Mackenzie asked, squinting at the ceiling of dark clouds, which were so low I thought I could touch them. "London would have shut down from this much snow. I'd say there's thirty-three centimetres at least and another twenty is expected over the next twenty-four hours."

"Darling Mac . . . um, I mean, Berkeley," Grandma said, giving her a nudge towards the sled. "The dogs and sleds are built for this."

"Yes, of course," Mackenzie said, but she didn't sound so sure.

"It will be fun," I reassured her. "It's much better than taking a stupid ol' car to the resort."

Grandma nodded her agreement. "I'm very proud of you both. Now mush!" she said, and mimed cracking a whip.

I greeted each dog attached to my sled with a stroke on the head while Mackenzie settled at the back of the sled closest to where the musher guy was standing ready to guide the dogs.

"Where are the seat belts?" Mackenzie asked.

"Just hold on tight," the musher told her. "You'll be fine."

"Thanks for letting me ride up front," I said, and plopped in front of Mackenzie. I wrapped the pile of blankets around us.

"You know the dogs don't stop to relieve themselves so if they need the loo they just go while they're running," Mackenzie said, and didn't even try to hide her smile.

"So you mean I'm in the poop line of fire?" I exclaimed.

She shrugged. "You wanted to do this."

"Hike!" the musher called and the dogs took off.

"Woohoo!" I shouted as we sped through the trees. The snowy landscape seemed to flash past frame by frame like an old-time movie. This didn't seem real: the wind stinging my cheeks; the trees stretching ice-covered branches towards us. The snow fell thicker and faster, creating a curtain of white as if we were flying into a dream world.

The musher was kissing the air to make the dogs go faster and faster.

Crack!

It took me a minute to register the sound. Had something broken on the sled?

We swerved to the left dangerously close to the

line of trees. The sled bumped over icy ground.

"Gee!" the musher yelled. The dogs pulled to the right.

Mackenzie wrapped her arms around me to keep us from flying off. My gloved fingers gripped the cord that stretched the tarp to the runners.

What was going on? I tried not to show my panic. If I freaked out then Mackenzie would be hysterical. Maybe this was normal for a dogsled ride.

The musher screamed. It wasn't a command. I looked back in time to see him tumble to the ground. The dogs didn't seem to notice; if anything it felt as if they were running faster without a musher to guide them.

We were on a runaway dogsled. If we didn't do something quickly, we were headed for an icy crash!

2

Mackenzie screamed. The sound must have upset the dogs because the team that had run in perfect synchronization shuddered and jerked but never slowed. "Ch-Chase ... wh-what..." she stammered in my ear and locked her hands at my chest.

"Hold on to the sled," I told Mackenzie. We were gaining on the sled ahead. I had to try to control our dogs

"Stop!" I shouted.

No response. The dogs raced faster and faster.

Trees whizzed by on either side, only an arm's length away.

"*Whoa*, that's the command to stop the dogs," Mackenzie said and then shouted, "Whoa!"

"Whoa!" We shouted at the top of our lungs, but it was no use. The dogs didn't respond.

The musher on the sled directly in front of us must have overheard. He glanced back; his mouth gaped open in shock.

"Watch out!" I yelled at him.

"Haw! Haw!" the musher commanded his dogsled and steered his team out of our way.

"Move! I can't stop! Watch out! Help!" Mackenzie and I screamed again and again as we passed the rest of the dogsleds. Each musher expertly manoeuvred their team away from us, but their faces contorted in shock and horror. Now I was freaking out.

"Chase! Mackenzie!" Grandma shrieked as we passed the final sled. She reached for us, but the musher held her back.

I was raised by my ex-United-States-Navy dad,

and he told me never to panic in an emergency. I took a deep breath and then another, trying to calm down. I looked back, hoping that one of the mushers would come after us, but the other sleds were already out of sight.

"Chase?!" Mackenzie's voice trembled with fear. She hugged me so tightly I thought she might squeeze me in two.

The dogs were trained for one purpose – to rocket through the icy tundra – and they showed no signs of stopping. We couldn't simply jump from the sled. With the trees so close, and at this speed, we would break every bone in our bodies.

Between the slushy spray from the dogs and the sled and the falling snow, I could barely see more than a few feet ahead of us. I gasped as we were spat from the forest and into an open field. Suddenly the dogs darted to the right. We bounced through fresh snow drifts. Had they seen a rabbit or a deer? Whatever it was now controlled our course.

"Think, Mackenzie," I shouted to her as I looked

around for something, anything to save us. "How do you slow this thing down?"

"Check the musher's pack!" Mackenzie yelled and pointed to the pouch attached to the sled. I could have kissed her. Great idea.

With painfully slow movements, I steadied myself then climbed over Mackenzie. The handlebar of the sled had broken off. That must have been the crack we heard and what made the musher fall. I spotted what I thought was a footbrake, but I was afraid what might happen if we stopped too suddenly.

The dogs began to bark and jerked to the left. I wrapped one arm around the top rail that ran from the back to the front of the sled and rummaged in the deerskin pouch that was tied right below the raw edges of the handlebar. Something shiny winked at me from the bottom of the pouch.

Please. Please. Please let it be. . .

"Yes!" I said as I pulled a knife from the bag.

The dogs' barking seemed to make the air and

my insides rattle. I dived to the front of the sled and pressed my body flat. I gripped the rope that tethered the dogs to the sled and began to saw. Almost immediately I could feel the rope give. Just a bit more and. . .

"Yeah!" we shouted as the dogs surged forward, and we slowed to a stop and flopped into the snow. My legs were shaking too badly to stand.

"I'm never travelling by dog, horse or even a hippo ever again," Mackenzie said, and crawled next to me.

We lay on our backs. The snowflakes looked like they were diving, not floating, towards us. "I hope the dogs will be OK," Mackenzie said as the barking faded away.

"I'm sure they'll find their way home," I said, sounding more sure than I was. I stuck out my tongue and let the icy drops coat it.

Mackenzie elbowed me in the ribs. "You like this, don't you?"

"What?"

"Action. Adventure." She said the words as if they were dirty.

I realized I was buzzing. It was the same feeling I got when I crossed any finish line or jumped a ditch a bit too wide and still made it across. I shrugged. "Yeah, so?"

"Does danger follow you everywhere you go?" she asked with a laugh.

I stood and pulled her to her feet. "You can't blame me for this." I showed her the broken handlebar. "I think that wood has been cut."

Mackenzie didn't look. "This was an accident."

"I think someone wanted the sled to crash."

"Don't be ridiculous. Look at this thing." She kicked the sled's runner. "It's ancient. The handlebar snapped because it was old and worn out."

"I'm not so sure."

Mackenzie planted her fists on her hips. "I know you've been bored. Planning a party isn't really your style but don't look for a mystery when there isn't one."

I didn't say it, but I wondered if this was another

attempt on Mackenzie's life. Had someone figured out she was alive?

"This isn't about me," Mackenzie insisted as if she'd read my mind. "We weren't supposed to be on the sled."

"OK, whatever," I said because I could see she was freaking out a little. I'd drop it for now, but I'd have to be more vigilant. "How are we going to get back to the resort?"

"We call for help," she said, as she removed her gloves and pulled her phone from the zipped pocket with the logo on the front of her snowsuit. "No reception!" she shrieked.

"Maybe we can retrace our route and find the others." I marched the way we came. We could be miles away from where we started. It was getting colder and the snow seemed to be coming down in sheets, not flakes. The dogs could have taken us closer to the resort or in the opposite direction. I had no idea. I stopped when I realized Mackenzie wasn't following.

"Mackenzie!" I shouted.

She raced past me. "If my calculations are correct, I think there's a cabin less than a mile this way."

"How could you possibly know that?" I said when I caught up to her.

"I studied a map of the resort," she said as if that's something everyone would do. "Don't you remember? They gave us one when we checked in."

"Yeah, but how do you know where we are and where it is exactly?"

"Well, I calculated our average speed and how many times and in which direction we turned, the route we were supposed to take and how long it should have taken us—"

"Yeah, yeah. OK, smarty pants, I believe you. Lead on!"

Within five minutes, we spotted a chimney above the tree line. In ten more minutes we were standing outside an old log cabin. I had to admit that having a geeky friend came in handy.

"What is this place?" I asked. My dad would have

called it rustic. That's what he called our zillion-year-old house in Indiana with its peeling paint and leaky roof.

"It's part of the Winter Wonder Resort. Guests can pay extra to stay in the middle of nowhere."

"Why would you pay more to stay in this old place when there's a big lodge with a roaring fire and non-stop, all-you-can-eat buffets?"

"Out here you have the best chance of seeing the Northern Lights."

My fingers and toes were tingling with cold. Even the thick, custom-designed gloves and boots the resort had loaned us had their limits. "Let's get inside and find a phone," I said and jiggled the door handle.

"Locked," Mackenzie said, and rubbed her arms. "We really do need to seek shelter. Based on the wind chill and at these temperatures, we could get frostbite on any exposed skin in ten to thirty minutes."

"Duh," I said. I didn't need her to tell me it was freaking cold. My nose hairs were beginning to freeze.

We raced around the cabin. Every door was locked up tight. We couldn't even smash a window because the windows were covered with wooden shudders. I tried to prise one open but with my gloved hands and fingers stiff from the cold, it was no use.

"Try your phone again," I said to Mackenzie.

She held her phone high in the air and walked around on her tiptoes. "Nothing."

"Maybe we need to get higher?" I pointed to the roof.

Mackenzie shook her head. "No, thanks. I prefer to freeze on the ground so my body won't shatter when I finally pass out from the cold."

I dragged her to the back of the cabin where I'd already spotted how we could climb to the roof.

"They will be looking for us. We don't need to do this," Mackenzie protested.

"Then we will be easy to spot from up there." I scrambled up a pile of wood that was stacked next to a shed. I hauled Mackenzie next to me. From there, it was only a matter of launching ourselves across a few feet to the rooftop. "See, nothing to it," I said when I reached the roof.

"How do you talk me into your crazy schemes?" She shrieked as she leaped for the roof. The top half of her body made it, but the bottom half dangled off the side. I grabbed the belt of her snowsuit and dragged her to safety.

"Wow," she sighed once we were safely perched on the roof's peak.

"Wow," I echoed as we took in the landscape.

The world around us was a hushed glittery white. The horizon glowed as the sunset painted the clouds what Crayola would call a neon-carrot orange. I loved everything about this snowy paradise, except the lack of daylight – and the fact we might freeze to death. This time of year there were only six hours of sunlight. How did people live with so little sunshine?

We checked our phones again. No signal. *Argh!*

"Maybe if we make noise they'll hear us before they can see us," she said, and fumbled with her phone. Her favourite song blared from the phone's tiny speakers. The sound seemed to fill every space in the forest. "We need to keep warm," she said. She planted her feet and started to sort of dance and sing at the top of her lungs and so did I. We must have looked ridiculous but neither one of us cared.

"It's like a painting," she said when the song ended.

"Amazing," I agreed, and then I saw something even more beautiful – two Winter Wonder snowmobiles racing to our rescue!

I should have been excited that I wasn't destined to be a human icicle, but something was bothering me. It was the same feeling I'd had when I'd arrived in the Maldives, that nagging sensation that something bad was brewing.

"We are saved," Mackenzie said, and wrapped her arm around me. "What is it? What's wrong?"

"Nothing." I tried to sound convincing.

"We aren't going to freeze to death. Why aren't you happy?"

"I am," I said.

"Chase. . ." Mackenzie said my name in a way that meant she knew something was wrong.

This place was cold in more ways than the low number on the thermometer. "Something's not right."

"Can't you relax and enjoy yourself?" she said.

"Yeah, sure," I said but I couldn't.

"It's your overactive imagination combined with the loss of feeling to your extremities," Mackenzie said with a playful punch.

I hoped she was right.

Grandma and Shauna were waiting outside the lodge when Mackenzie and I returned from our snowy adventure. Grandma didn't say a word, just hugged us.

"Are you all right?" Shauna asked, piling in on the hug. "What happened out there?"

"All that matters is that my girls are unharmed." Grandma's words were muffled because she was still hugging us so tightly, and her face was smushed against our snowsuits.

"What about the dogs and the musher?" I

asked, trying to wriggle free of the group hug, but Grandma wouldn't let go. "Are they OK?"

"The dogs have been reunited with their musher," Shauna said. "I'm so sorry this happened. I was assured that the dogsled teams were the best in the area."

"Never mind," Grandma said, almost pushing us away. She wiped at her eyes. "We've got work to do. Shauna, how are the final preparations coming for the party in the ice pub tonight?"

"Absolutely, one-hundred-and-fifty percent under control!" Shauna must have been a cheerleader in a past life because when she was in full-on event-planner mode she spoke in exclamation marks. "I'm glad my two best assistants are OK! See you later!" Shauna bounced across the snowy courtyard towards the ice hotel and pub. The resort constructed a hotel, church, pub, maze and loads of sculptures every year using ice from the nearby lake. It would melt over the summer, and then they would start again the next winter. That was pretty amazing but also pretty weird.

"Maybe you girls should rest for a while," Grandma said, leading us into the lodge. We surrounded the massive stone fireplace in the middle of the lobby. The warmth of the roaring fire was almost overwhelming after nearly freezing to death. We unzipped our snowsuits and removed our gloves. I wasn't sure I'd ever feel my fingers again.

"We are fine, Ariadne, really," Mackenzie replied, although the fluffy cushions seemed to swallow her as she collapsed into one of the lobby's many overstuffed couches. "According to the itinerary, Chase and I are supposed to be delivering gift bags." If she read things once or twice, she remembered them. She was worse than Shauna about the itinerary. "Where are the gift bags?"

"They are in my room," Grandma said.

"I'll get them," Mackenzie said, springing to her feet. Grandma handed her the key card, and she dashed off. Since we arrived, Mackenzie was always doing things like that.

"She doesn't always need to be working," Grandma muttered.

"She thinks she owes you," I explained. Mackenzie's life had been threatened when she lived in London with her mother. Because Mackenzie's mum and my mom had been childhood friends, Grandma had agreed to act as Mackenzie's guardian and hide her in the Maldives to keep her safe. That hadn't worked very well. We caught the baddies who were after Mackenzie in the Maldives, but we still didn't know who the mastermind behind it all was.

"I am happy to look after that lovely girl." Grandma watched Mackenzie disappear on to the elevator. "Her mum has always been a good friend to me."

Now was my chance. It was the first time I'd been alone with Grandma for days, and she was in a sentimental mood instead of the drill sergeant she sometimes was when it came to her business. "Um, Gran," I started. I'd decided I wanted to contact my long-lost mom, and Grandma was the only one who could help me. In the Maldives, I'd discovered why my mom had never been part of my life. She was in prison. I'd been born there. That's why my dad and grandma never, ever mentioned her. I was kind of, sort of getting used to the idea of my criminal mom. "I thought I might like to—"

Grandma interrupted. "When you drop off the bags at the ice hotel can you check that the ice sculptures are finished?" She was examining her itinerary.

"Yeah, sure, but I wondered if you might have—" I gulped.

"And the rooms; Shauna said some of the beds needed to be rebuilt," she added, rifling through the pages on her clipboard, not noticing that I desperately was trying to ask her something.

"Mackenzie and I will check." I needed to say this quickly. My courage was thawing faster than my toes. Everybody only gets one bio mom, and I was ready to know more about mine. "I was thinking I would like to. . ."

She looked at me at last. "Go snowmobiling?"

"No, it's not about that."

"Cross-country skiing? That's on the itinerary

for later in the weekend."

"No. I mean, yes, but what I was hoping you could tell me was. . ."

She squinted at me. "Go on."

My mom's email address, I said it over and over in my head but the words wouldn't form on my lips.

"Ready, Chase?" Mackenzie called from the lodge door with fists full of shiny blue gift bags exploding with silver tissue paper. We'd helped Shauna assemble them last night.

"Chase?" Grandma said. "What did you want to ask me?"

I couldn't do it, not like this with Mackenzie breathing down my neck and Grandma staring at me as if I was a pink rhino with fairy wings.

"Nothing," I said, and gave Grandma a kiss on the cheek. She'd worried about me enough for one day.

I grabbed some of the gift bags from Mackenzie. "Did you ask her?" she whispered.

I shook my head. "Not the right time."

"It's never the right time," she muttered. I knew she was right.

I yanked open the large wooden lodge door. "Whoa!" I sort of screamed and stumbled backwards.

Identical twin boys were framed in the doorway. They had straight brown hair that was too long to be short and too short to be long. They were tall and thin with skin so white it looked like it had never even seen a picture of the sun. Two identical black wheelie suitcases bookended the boys.

"Welcome," Mackenzie said, and nudged me aside. "I'm Ma — " she started but caught her mistake. "I'm Berkeley and this is Chase. Are you here for the launch of Love Late in Life?"

The boys smirked. "How old do you think we are?" the one on the left said. They looked our age, maybe a little older. "We're here—" Right Twin started but was interrupted by his brother, "We are on a break from our boarding school." They had British accents like Mackenzie. "Yes, yes, that's right," Right Twin said.

"I thought we had reserved the entire resort for the launch," I said to Mackenzie. She shrugged.

"We, um, come here the same time every year. We promised to stay out of your way and take one of the staff rooms in the lodge—"

Left Twin interrupted his brother. "I'm Taylor and that's Toby, but everyone calls us TnT, like, short for dynamite." They were staring at Mackenzie as if I wasn't even in the room.

Mackenzie nervously giggled at their lame joke. She cocked her head and twisted one of her perfect reddish-brown curls around her finger. Was my shy, awkward, geeky friend actually flirting? Did flirting come naturally to all pretty people? I tried to laugh too, just to be nice, but my forced laughter sounded like a half-cough, half-bark.

"I went to boarding school in the UK," Mackenzie said. Did she bat her eyes at them? I elbowed her, not only to make her stop flirting, but also to remind her that she was presumed dead. She wasn't supposed to tell people where she was from.

"What school do you attend?" I asked the boys, not that I knew the names of any posh British schools.

"Ingenium International College," Left Twin said. I couldn't remember if it was Taylor or Toby.

That school name sounded familiar for some reason.

"There's a party later and then we're going to see the Northern lights," Mackenzie said, flirting again. "You are welcome to join us—"

"Yeah, maybe we'll see you around," I interrupted. "We've got work to do."

"Toodles, TnT," Mackenzie said with a giggle as I dragged her out of the lodge.

In the centre of the courtyard stood a huge block of ice. It was twice my height and had the Winter Wonder Resort logo – a series of snowflakes and wavy lines that I thought were supposed symbolize the Northern Lights, not that we'd seen them yet. When we passed it, I shouted "Race ya!" and took off. I reached the ice hotel first. I always beat Mackenzie.

"I wish you wouldn't do that," Mackenzie said

between pants, trying to catch her breath.

"Do you want to time ourselves to see how fast we can deliver the gift bags?" I asked.

"No," she replied. "I want to look at the rooms properly. The last time we were here, Sven was still making improvements."

"Grandma wants us to check to make sure everything's finished." I could be business-like too. We jumped when a chainsaw roared to life. "That's Sven," I reassured Mackenzie. I'd watched him carve a life-sized angel from a hunk of ice using a chainsaw yesterday. He was a Boy Wonder when it came to ice. He was only seventeen and the featured artist for this year's ice hotel. I loved watching him work.

We walked down the main corridor that was lined with huge ice columns. The grinding noise of the chainsaw stopped as abruptly as it had started. Ice chandeliers clattered above our heads. Mackenzie read off the guests' names, and I placed the right bag in the centre of the bed, which was made one hundred per cent of ice and covered with moose or deer pelts.

Mackenzie was like a walking Wikipedia of fun facts. "Did you know there are more than sixty rooms that cover more than six thousand square metres?"

"Nope," I said with a shrug. "Did you know that blue slushies are the best flavour and rainbow Snow Cones look great but taste gross?"

Her eyebrows scrunched together, making her *you're crazy* face, but she continued as if she was my own personal tour guide. "The Winter Wonder Resort uses about forty-eight thousand cubic metres of snice – that's snow and ice – and nearly two thousand tonnes of ice to create the hotel, maze, pub and cathedral."

"How do you know all this?"

"Didn't you listen when Mr Ashworth gave us the tour?" she asked. I shrugged again. Obviously not. "I also did some research on the Internet."

Of course you did.

Each room had a different theme. One was an icy garden. Another was decorated with large and small snowflakes. Another had a huge ice bird sitting on a nest of snowball eggs. Some were more abstract with coloured lights illuminating random shapes carved from ice. "This is my favourite," I told Mackenzie as we approached the room with the angel. I could hear the clink and tap of Sven at work inside.

"This is the last gift bag." She handed it to me.

"Hey, Sven!" I said, and almost dropped the bag in what looked like a big paddling pool framed with blocks of ice.

"Hi, Chase." He removed his goggles. "I am nearly finished," he said with his lovely Swedish accent. "I made the frame and now all I have to do is fill the bed with water. It is easier than dragging blocks of ice from the lake."

"Wow, that's amazing," I said when I noticed that he had added to the sculpture. The angel was now perched on a tower of halos.

"Wait." He reached down and flicked a switch, which gave the halos a golden glow.

"Wow," Mackenzie sighed behind me. "That's. . ."

"Yeah. . ." I agreed; there were no words.

"I am glad you like," he said, and went back to work. "I have some final touches to make. I told Shauna that I may not be done with this room and the one next door tonight."

"I'll leave this here for now," I told him and set the gift bag on the round ice table. "See you later, Sven."

"Come on," Mackenzie said. "We need to get dressed for the party." She was doing this weird race-walking thing.

"What's your hurry?" I asked as I followed her down the corridor.

"Don't you think it's a bit creepy in here?"

I shrugged. The sun had nearly set and the chandeliers hadn't been switched on yet. The ice sculptures, which gleamed during the day, made eerie shadows in the dark. The sculpture of a little child with big blue stones for eyes had looked playful in the daylight; now the kid looked a bit demonic. Maybe she was right.

When I caught up to her, I paused. "Did you hear

that?" I whipped around, but no one was behind us. The corridor was empty.

"Stop that. It's not funny," Mackenzie whined, and touched the jagged scar on her neck, the scar she'd received in London the second time someone tried to kill her. She did that when she was nervous.

"No, listen." I held her still. There it was again. "It sounded like footsteps," I whispered.

She glared at me. Sure, I loved to spook her. I'd hide and jump out at her when I got the chance, but I'd really heard something. We took a few steps. Mackenzie suddenly stopped. This time she'd heard it too.

"Follow me," I whispered in my quietest voice right next to her ear. We tiptoed to the next room and slipped inside. The architects of the ice hotel could make chandeliers and ridiculously detailed art from ice, but they hadn't found a way to make doors inside the icy buildings. The hotel rooms only had curtains, which wasn't much protection. The footsteps were getting closer and louder. Someone was stalking us!

4

The thud of our stalker's footsteps echoed in my pounding heart and Mackenzie's panicked panting. I wasn't going to wait here helpless. I whispered my plan to Mackenzie. She frantically shook her head, but it was time for action whether she liked it or not.

I gauged the direction of the footsteps and slipped beside the doorway so I would be ready, but out of sight. I had to time this just right. Mackenzie was slowly making her way behind me.

I held up my gloved hand and counted down. Three . . . two . . . one. . .

"AAAHHH!" we shrieked as we sprang from hiding.

"AAAHHH!" our stalkers squealed in reply. Two figures in Winter Wonder Resort snowsuits darted in opposite directions, skidding on the snowy floor until they wiped out in a cartoon-like fashion. They were scrambling to their feet, but they couldn't get any traction in the clunky snow boots. The moment after I surprised them like some rabid polar bear I realized who they were – TnT.

I shouldn't have, but I laughed. They slipped and slid in a panic as they tried to escape. I wished I'd filmed it because it would have been one of the funniest blooper videos ever. The boys were crawling away.

"Hey! Wait!" I called to them. "TnT, we're sorry."

I rushed to one of the twins while Mackenzie helped the other.

"Why'd you do that?" my twin asked me. I'd have to figure out a way to tell them apart.

"We thought someone was following us," I said.

"We weren't following you," the other twin

replied. "We were checking out the ice hotel. And that's a strange response to being followed."

"You don't know what we've been through," Mackenzie said but then pinned her lips shut tightly. We couldn't talk about our adventure in the Maldives because Mackenzie wasn't supposed to have survived it. She was a terrible liar, which was a good trait in a friend but a horrible trait for a spy.

"What she means is it's creepy in here, don't you think?" I interjected. I didn't want them to ask any questions. "We didn't mean to scare you."

The boys smirked at each other. "You better watch out," one said. "Yeah, because sooner or later we will pay you back," the other twin finished his sentence and then they raced away.

"You really know how to make friends," Mackenzie said when they disappeared around the corner. "Danger isn't looming at every turn." She frowned. "Well, I guess it is now."

"Welcome to the Winter Wonder Resort!" Mr Ashworth, the resort manager, was standing on the ice stage in the centre of the pub, shouting to the gathering crowd. Red twinkle lights outlined the room. Ice hearts dangled from the ceiling. Shauna had done an amazing job of bring the *Melting Your Hearts* theme to life for the VIP party. Strange to see everyone dressed for the outside when we were inside, sort of. The ice pub was basically a big igloo with everything – even the glasses – constructed of ice. Everyone was wearing the black-and-blue snowsuits, boots and gloves issued by the Winter Wonder Resort.

Mackenzie and I replaced Shauna at the welcome table. It had taken Mackenzie an hour and a half to get ready, including ironing her red silk thermals. We shared a room, and I had been amazed how long it took for her curls to look perfectly messy. I achieved the same just-out-of-bed effect by simply waking up.

"I'm thrilled to see so many old friends and Ingenium International College alumni," Mr Ashworth said, and held both hands straight in the air. That's where I'd heard that school name before. TnT went there and so did a number of our guests.

Several members of the crowd mimicked Mr Ashworth as if it had been choreographed and shouted, "I! I!" It must be some weird college ritual.

"I, I indeed," he replied. "Thanks to Ariadne for allowing me to invite a few of my fellow board members and their grandchildren." He paused and with a goofy grin, waved at Lucinda Sterling. Alexia was standing next to her grandmother and rolled her eyes melodramatically. "I hope you have a wonderful time in my winter wonderland. Ariadne has quite the weekend planned for you. I also hope you'll consider investing in her app. The pensioner market. . ."

He droned on about money stuff. Mackenzie and I had heard it all before. Grandma needed a few investors to take her app global. Tonight was for the VIPs. Tomorrow the rest of the guests would arrive.

Mackenzie organized the rows of folders with

the Love Late in Life logo while I carved my initials in the ice table with the tip of a Love Late in Life pen. She frowned and shook her head disapprovingly.

"Don't be such a goody two-shoes," I muttered and removed my glove. I pressed my warm palm on the table and melted away my graffiti. Mackenzie returned to her alphabetizing.

"Let me add my sincere gratitude. . ." Grandma had taken the stage in her bright red snowsuit. Everyone watched her. It wasn't just what she was wearing or the sparkle in her voice; she was mesmerizing. "I invited you to bring your grandchildren because I was only recently introduced to mine." She gestured to me and Mackenzie.

I waved. "Wave," I whispered to Mackenzie. She had forgotten that we were pretending to be cousins.

Grandma continued, "I'm beginning to understand the joys of being a grandparent."

And I was enjoying being a granddaughter. I just wanted to get to know my mom too.

"Excuse me," a red-headed girl said as she stepped up to the welcome table.

"Oh, hi!" I said, remembering that I was supposed to be on duty. "I mean, welcome to the launch of Love Late in Life. What's your name?"

"I'm Katrina Memering," she replied. "Sorry I'm so late. My flight was delayed."

I searched the folders for grandchildren but her name wasn't there. That can't be right. I double-checked the grandchildren's packets myself. "What's your grandparent's name?"

She blushed. "I'm not here as a guest," she explained. "I'm a freelance writer. Shauna hired me to write a feature story on the new app for a pensioner magazine."

"You don't look old enough to be a reporter," I said. The filter in my brain that was supposed to keep me from blurting my stupid thoughts often malfunctioned.

"Sorry about my rude friend," Mackenzie said, and handed her the press folder with her name on it.

"I get that a lot," Katrina said. "I skipped a few grades."

"Can we introduce you to a few people?" I gave her a snowsuit, boots and gloves.

"That would be great," Katrina said with a smile and a flip of her long red hair. She was one of those people who looked pretty average until she smiled.

"That's Ariadne, my grandma and the founder of Love Late in Life." I pointed to the stage. "I'll introduce you to her later."

"I've read a lot about her," Katrina said. "Impressive CV."

I nodded.

"You should meet Shauna," Mackenzie said and looked in Shauna's direction. Alexia had her cornered. Shauna's head was bowed so her blonde hair half covered her face. Alexia's mouth was moving and her eyes were rolling so she must be complaining. Poor Shauna. "Shauna is occupied, but I'd be happy to introduce you to—"

"Um, on second thought." Katrina turned away.

"I'm really tired. Jet-lagged, you know. Maybe I will go to my room instead."

"U-uh, O-OK," I stammered, confused by her quick change. She looked sort of nervous all of a sudden. "You will find your room number and key in your packet."

"You won't want to miss the Northern Lights excursion later," Mackenzie called after her. Katrina was almost running away now.

"Is it my imagination or is everyone acting weird?" I whispered to Mackenzie. She shrugged.

The presentations were over and music started to play. Shauna had let Mackenzie and me make the playlist. Grandma and Shauna talked to everyone, smiling and nodding and making the guests smile and laugh. That was not a talent I had – nor wanted to have. Parties like this were not my style.

"I'm starving," Mackenzie said. "I'll get us some food from the buffet."

"Good idea."

The moment she left I got that *being watched*

feeling. I scanned the room. TnT were nowhere to be seen. Maybe Mackenzie was right. I was being paranoid, but I couldn't shake it. I looked around again. This time I spotted the source of my paranoia. Someone in a silvery snowsuit was lurking in a corner at the far side of the room. He – or was it a she – ducked behind a cluster of guests. I shifted so I could keep my eye on whoever it was. The person's hood was up so I couldn't see his or her face.

Mackenzie was weaving through the crowd, holding a plate piled high with food. For someone her size, she could sure eat. I waved at her to hurry up.

"I got you some buffalo wings." She placed the plate on the table between us. She knew me well, the hotter and spicier the better.

"Look!" I said and positioned her so she was looking straight at the figure in the silver snowsuit.

"What?" She wriggled out of my grasp. "I'm hungry." She forked a meatball and plopped it in her mouth.

"Someone's watching us," I said but the figure had disappeared. Mackenzie rolled her eyes. "No, really, right over there. Someone was wearing a silver snowsuit—" Mackenzie shut me up by shoving a firecracker prawn in my mouth.

"Stop imagining mysteries." She devoured the last meatball from the plate.

"What about the mystery of the disappearing meatballs?" I laughed. She was right. I was letting my overactive imagination run wild. No one was going to find Mackenzie here, and there was no other reason anyone would be stalking us.

"May I have your attention?!" Shauna stepped on to the stage with some help from Mr Ashworth. "I've been informed that the Northern Lights have been spotted and the conditions are perfect!"

"I am not going outside," Alexia shrieked. "It's too cold. It's only lights. What's the big deal?"

I'd known Alexia for an afternoon, and I already intensely disliked her. If you searched *spoiled rotten brat* on the internet, I was sure her picture would pop up.

"You don't have to go, darling." Lucinda fussed over her granddaughter. "Let's not make a scene. I'm sure you can go to your room, if you'd rather."

"And that's another thing," Alexia shouted. "Under no circumstances am I sleeping on a block of ice on a smelly deer skin. Disgusting."

Most people would kill for this vacation, and she was pouting. And what I hated more than spoiled brats was the fact that Mr Ashworth, Grandma and Shauna were racing over to her aid. If it were up to me, I'd freeze her in a block of ice.

"I'm sure Serena here—" Lucinda wrapped her arm around Shauna.

"It's Shauna," she corrected.

"I'm sure Shauna will take good care of you, won't you, dear?" Lucinda cooed at Shauna. I clenched my fists and hoped Shauna wouldn't give in.

"I would be happy to sort out a deluxe suite in the lodge for Alexia," Mr Ashworth piped up.

"Thank you, darling," Lucinda said, patting him on his full round face.

The Alexia show was over. She stormed away, and Mr Ashworth scuttled after.

"Follow me! You won't want to miss this once-in-a-lifetime light show!" Shauna said, cranking her smile to full wattage. Everyone filed out of the ice pub.

I ate a few wings before we headed into the cold. Mackenzie clapped her gloved hands. "Come on! Come on! I've been dying to see the Northern Lights. We are very lucky. You can't predict when and where the Northern Lights — also known as the aurora borealis – will appear."

I licked my fingers clean. "Uh-huh," I mumbled. Mackenzie was in full-on geek mode.

"The Northern Lights are created when gaseous particles collide," she continued. "The Earth's atmosphere and charged particles from the sun to be exact..." She dashed off, but never stopped yakking about how the colour of the display is based on which gas is present or something like that.

Grandma, playing the good hostess, was at the back of the crowd, making sure everyone was heading in the right direction. I fell in line beside her.

"Thanks for your help, Chase," Grandma said and took my hand. This was nice. I slowed my pace.

"I want to contact my mom," I blurted. The thought sort of snuck up on me and slipped out.

Grandma stopped. I had clearly caught her off-guard. "Not now." She squeezed my hand. "Some day when you're older. Isn't it enough that we are getting to know each other? Let's enjoy this wonderful opportunity."

I didn't know if she meant the Northern Lights, faintly glimmering over the frozen lake ahead, or the two of us together at last. "Yeah, OK, sure," I said, but it wasn't really OK. My dad and grandma had kept my mom a secret from me my whole life, but I was determined to know more whether they liked it or not.

"Gather around!" Shauna called. "This clearing is the perfect place for viewing. The resort has constructed a few snow benches around the lake. Please don't venture too far on to the lake. It may not be completely frozen. Enjoy the show!"

"Over here!" Mackenzie called to Grandma and me.

"You go ahead," Grandma said. "I need to finalize plans for tomorrow."

"Is everything OK?" I asked.

She nodded. "More guests tomorrow. I need to check the itineraries." She sounded tired. "Enjoy the Northern Lights. See you tomorrow at lunch. You and Mackenzie are hosting the activities for the grandchildren, which start right after everyone's eaten."

"Got it!" I dived into place next to Mackenzie.

With everyone wearing the same snowsuits, I couldn't tell who was who. Groups of people gathered along the bank of the lake. A few people dared to slip and slide further on the frozen water. A couple wandered off into the forest, which was strange. They wouldn't see the lights from there.

We flopped on our backs and stared at the night sky. At first only faint lines of greenish-yellow light swept through the air. I squinted. Was that all there was? It wasn't as cool as fireworks or even the laser light show at the state park.

"It still feels weird to be in the Arctic Circle," I said. We'd travelled more than five thousand miles from the Maldives, and the temperature change was unbelievable – something like an eighty-five degree drop in temperature. That's swimsuits to parkas. I still couldn't believe this was my life.

The Northern Lights rolled in waves of colour – greens but also pinks and purples. I gasped as the night sky came alive. The air felt electric. I'd seen pictures of the lights but that was nothing like the real thing. It was so stunning, it made me forget for a minute or two that I was forbidden to contact my very own mom.

We lay there open-mouthed until the lights eventually whispered away.

"Wow," I breathed.

"Amazing," Mackenzie replied. We didn't move, didn't want to break the spell.

I should have been more vigilant. It always

happens when you least expect it, when you've let your guard down.

I didn't hear anyone coming. One minute we were gazing at the most astounding light display and then the next minute. . .

Splat!

5

The first snowball splattered dead centre on my face. The next walloped Mackenzie in the gut. I wiped away the slush as we jumped to our feet. The snowballs relentlessly thudded against us accompanied by the distinct sound of laughter.

"Oi!" Mackenzie bellowed. "Stop! Cut it out!" Each direct hit stung even through the snowsuit. Mackenzie covered her head, twisting and turning with each strike, but I zoomed in on the source of our attack.

TnT were standing only twenty feet away with a

pile of snowballs at their feet.

"Payback time!" one shouted and lobbed a huge snowball right at me. I dodged out of the way, but it smacked Mackenzie and knocked her down.

"Counter-attack?" she asked. Her face was tight with anger.

"Abso-freaking-lutely," I whispered. We huddled together as if in defeat while TnT continued their assault. We quickly made a few snowballs and packed them tightly. "You make the ammo and I'll shoot."

"Not a chance," Mackenzie leaped to her feet, took aim and threw. The snowball rocketed towards the boys and scored a direct hit.

"Impressive," I told Mackenzie, who was grinning from ear to ear.

The boys were stunned by our accuracy and force. We synchronized our attack so while one packed a snowball the other launched her icy ammo.

"Cut it out!" one yelled. "That's enough!" the other shrieked as they bolted to the lodge.

"Payback!" I shouted my reply. We chased them, pelting them with snowballs when we could.

They dived behind the big ice block bearing the resort logo which sat in the centre of the courtyard. We had them right where we wanted them. We stopped to create an armload of snowballs. I directed Mackenzie around one side, and I would attack from the other. We tiptoed to the sculpture.

"Surprise!" TnT shouted and pelted us with a flurry of snowballs. Too late we spotted the stockpile they must have made before they'd attacked us at the lake. TnT were worthy opponents. I was impressed. We retreated, turned our backs and accepted our pummelling.

"You win!" I said.

"We surrender!" Mackenzie echoed.

One final snowball splattered on the top of my head.

"That will teach to you mess with TnT," one twin said.

Someone flung open the lodge's front doors

and staggered forward. "You've got to help me!" We recognized the face under the hood of the snowsuit – Alexia. What was it now? Not enough bubbles in her bubble bath? Too much foam in her cappuccino?

"Thank heavens I've found you," she said breathlessly.

"What's the matter?" I asked without an ounce of warmth or sincerity.

"She's gone," Alexia said. "Vanished."

"Who?" Mackenzie asked with similar disinterest.

"My grandmother, Lucinda," Alexia said as if we were the dumbest people on the planet.

"Have you tried to call her?" Mackenzie asked.

"Did you check her room?" I added.

"Yes, of course I did," Alexia replied. "She doesn't answer, and I can't find anyone around."

"We'll help you look for her." I gestured to indicate me and the boys, but the boys had disappeared. They must have met Alexia before. I didn't blame them for saving themselves from another of her dramas. "I'm sure Mrs Sterling simply is taking advantage of everything that the Winter Wonder Resort has to offer." I couldn't help making a little dig about Alexia's refusal to go on the dogsleds or see the Northern Lights or sleep in the ice hotel.

She huffed and rolled her eyes. When I made a horrible face, my dad always told me it would freeze that way. Alexia rarely had a nice expression so maybe her face had already frozen. I smiled at my private joke.

"What? Are you going to just stand here or are you going to help?" Snotty Central said. "Is everyone around here incompetent?" She probably never heard another of my dad's sayings: *You catch more flies with honey than vinegar.*

I opened my mouth to tell her exactly what I thought of her, but Mackenzie grabbed my arm. "Why don't I help you look, Alexia? Chase can go and tell Shauna and Ariadne. I'm sure we will find her."

I mouthed *thank you* to Mackenzie and darted off.

I checked my watch. It was nearly one a.m. I didn't

want to bother my grandma unless I absolutely had to. She had looked exhausted earlier, and I was sure Alexia was being a drama queen.

I tapped on Shauna's door. She was on the ground floor in the room nearest to the lobby. Our room was next door. Grandma had an executive suite on the top floor. I hated to wake Shauna, but she had told Mackenzie and me to let her handle any tricky situations. No answer. I tapped again. Nothing. I unzipped my snowsuit because I was starting to sweat.

"Who's there?" Shauna's voice asked through the door when I finally removed my gloves and knocked properly.

"It's me. It's Chase."

The door opened a few inches. "What's wrong?" she asked. She was wearing one of the Winter Wonder Resort's fluffy bathrobes. Her cheeks were red and chapped.

"It's Alexia." I went to push the door open, but she held it fast. I accidentally touched her hand. It was cold.

"What's she done now?" Shauna asked.

"She can't find Lucinda. She says she's missing. Berkeley is helping her look, but maybe we should call the police or ask security to search?"

Shauna sighed. "Mrs Sterling asked for a night at the Northern Lights cabin tonight. Maybe she didn't tell Alexia or maybe that diva forgot. Mrs Sterling said she needed some time to herself." Shauna raised her eyebrows as if to say we both knew why.

"I can understand that," I said.

"Alexia is a nightmare."

"I'll tell her not to worry."

"Would you? I can't face another drama with that spoiled girl," Shauna said. "You and Berkeley should get to bed. We've got a big day tomorrow. I don't want you to waste another minute on babysitting that brat."

"No problem," I said, a bit surprised at Shauna's reaction. I'd never heard her say a single bad word against anyone. In planning the weekend with so many tiny details and Grandma's insistence that everything was perfect, I'd never seen Shauna lose her temper. She was usually so patient. Alexia clearly had a negative effect on everyone.

"Did you and Berkeley get the message I left you at the front desk?"

I shook my head.

"I'm really sorry, but Sven didn't finish the ice hotel rooms. Once we'd checked in the VIPs, there wasn't one left for you. I'm really sorry, maybe another night." And with that she eased her door shut. I was disappointed. I'd been looking forward to sleeping in the ice hotel.

I called Mackenzie and updated her. I could hear Alexia shouting and carrying on when Mackenzie relayed the message.

Fifteen minutes later Mackenzie joined me in our room. I was already snuggled into bed and sort of glad that it wasn't a block of ice. "That girl is evil," Mackenzie said. "She acted as if it was my fault her grandmother had made other plans."

"Don't you think it's strange that Mrs Sterling didn't tell Alexia she was going to be away for the night?" I asked. "Grandma wouldn't leave us like that."

"But we aren't as horrible as Alexia," she said.

"Agreed," I said, but something didn't feel right. I didn't say anything to Mackenzie as she changed into her pyjamas and crawled into bed. She'd say I was paranoid again. Maybe she was right; after everything that happened in the Maldives I was a bit jumpy. Nearly dying like a dozen times is bound to change you.

Now I was wide awake. I walked over to the window and drew back the curtain. The moon made the snow sparkle. I was so lucky. Not many kids my age travelled to the Arctic Circle or rode in a dogsled – especially a runaway one – and saw those amazing ice sculptures. I glanced at the sky and was sure I saw a faint swirling of the Northern Lights.

Movement in the forest nearby caught my eye. I scanned the landscape. Maybe it was a wolf. Then I spotted a human-shaped figure moving through the trees. It stopped and appeared to look directly at me. I gasped. With the hood up and at this distance, I couldn't see a face.

"You OK?" Mackenzie asked half asleep.

"I'm fine. Go back to sleep."

When I looked out of the window again, the figure was gone.

6

"Seriously?" I said with a groan when the *click-clack* of Mackenzie's typing penetrated the pillow I'd pressed over my head. "What time is it?"

"I was trying to be quiet," Mackenzie replied.

"You failed." I chucked my pillow at her. She batted it away and clumsily flipped her laptop closed. I hadn't known her very long, but I could tell when she was hiding something. "What's so important that you're up so early?" I hopped out of bed.

"It's not that early," she said and placed her hands protectively on top of her computer.

"Not what I asked." I flopped next to her on the couch.

She hugged the laptop to her chest. She loved the new super-everything laptop Grandma had given her but not that much.

"Mackenzie, you're not contacting your mom, are you? It's not safe. We don't know who might be watching her or listening in." I remembered the dark figure staring at our window last night.

"I miss her." Her eyes filled with tears. Mackenzie's mum was pretty much the opposite of mine. She worked for the Royal Protection Command. She used to guard Prince Arthur, heir to the British throne, but now she worked behind the scenes.

"I know." I handed her the silver tissue box from a nearby table. "My dad told her that you were alive. He's been calling her once a week on a secure line with updates. When I spoke to him a few days ago, he said that she was fine and sent her love to you."

"We used to speak every day." She blew her nose.

"It must be difficult." Dad and I didn't talk that often, but I couldn't imagine not knowing when I'd speak to him again. I frowned. She'd almost made me forget she was up to something. "What were you doing on your computer?"

"I wasn't emailing anyone. I wouldn't do that. I don't have a death wish."

"Then what?" I tugged the computer out of her hands. She didn't stop me when I flipped it open. She typed in her password, and an old article from a British news organization popped on to the screen.

"I know you've been searching for your mum," Mackenzie said, and scooted a bit further away from me. "I've been researching her too."

"What?" Anger flashed through me. How dare she research my mom behind my back?

Our moms were childhood friends but their friendship ended when Mackenzie's mum had somehow helped send my mom to prison. I didn't want their war to become ours.

"I thought maybe if you knew more about your

mum. . ." She couldn't look at me. "If you could contact her—"

I interrupted. "And tell her not to kill you?" I couldn't believe I'd said that. Mackenzie's eyes were wide with shock. Grandma had told me that she feared my mom might be the mastermind behind the plot to hurt Mackenzie. I never, ever believed that was true. Well, not really.

"She can't hurt me from prison," she whispered. "My mum thinks Prince Arthur was behind the attacks on me – even if we can't prove it." How horrible to think your very own father was trying to kill you. Mackenzie had never met him. She didn't want anything to do with him or his royalness. "I know what it's like not to know one of your parents. I can't contact mine but I thought at least you might be able to contact yours."

Now I felt like the most awful person in the entire universe. "Sorry," I said. Maybe with her mad computer skills, she'd have better luck. All I knew about my mom was that her first name was Beatrice and that she was serving a life sentence.

"What did you find out?"

"Not a lot really. I searched using your grandma's and then your father's last names."

"I don't think my parents were ever married."

"It was worth a go."

"Thanks for trying." I handed the computer back, but she pushed it in my direction.

"I did find something when I searched Ariadne Sinclair. It's taken me loads of time to troll through years and years of web hits. Someone should write her biography. I found fourteen different companies she's been associated with or started. She volunteered for pretty much everything. There was a ton of information on her professional life. Ariadne is pretty protective about her private life though. Someone had deleted that section on her Wikipedia page and removed any references to her family from the Internet."

"Can you do that?"

"If you've got enough money and technical skills." She started to explain how to do it.

I didn't care about the how, I wanted to know

the what. "So. . ."

"I found a line or two on a gossip site with rumours about Ariadne and this lead singer. Have you ever hear of the punk band—?"

"What about my mom?"

"Just read." Mackenzie scrolled down a bit to an article with a date from the 1990s.

The headline was like a punch in the gut: *London Teen Killed by Drink Driver.* The girl was only fifteen years old. How terrible! I read on, but the article didn't name any names. "What does this have to do with Grandma?"

"That's only the first." A few clicks and Mackenzie pulled up another article. "This is the last."

The next article was about how a man, who had been charged with but not convicted of killing Elizabeth Sinclair, died under mysterious circumstances. The article said the sister of the deceased girl was questioned about the man's death but never charged. There was a quote from Ariadne, begging the police and reporters to leave her family alone. I was overwhelmed with sadness. I couldn't read any more, couldn't speak. I placed the computer on the glass-topped coffee table.

"I never knew Ariadne had two daughters," Mackenzie continued even though I didn't want to hear any more. "I can't imagine what it must have been like to lose a child that way."

Elizabeth. She was my mom's younger sister and would have been my aunt. Then the other part of the news story sank in. "Are you saying that my mom avenged her sister's death?"

"Nothing came of it, but the article implies that," Mackenzie said.

"What else did you find out?" I clicked on the browser history. I flicked from page to page.

"No matter how hard I try, I can't find anything about Beatrice's incarceration," Mackenzie said.

"I still can't believe my mom's in prison." I swallowed hard. I'd forced Grandma to tell me why my mom went to prison. I still found it difficult to accept that someone who shared my genes had killed people.

We stared at the computer screen. "You know you aren't your mum," she said after a long pause.

I was about to say that I knew that. Of course, I knew that. What a stupid thing to say! The awkward silence in our room was shattered by shouting coming from outside. We raced to the window and opened the curtains wide enough so we could see but not too wide that whoever was outside would notice. Two snow-suited figures were shouting and shoving each other. I wanted to know what they were saying. I reached for the window latch, but Mackenzie batted my hand away and shook her head like crazy. We were so close that her curls whipped my cheek.

Mackenzie nudged me away from the window. "It's rude to listen in on other people's private conversations."

"It's rude to argue outside people's windows."

"They probably think everyone is staying in the ice hotel."

If I didn't do something quickly the fight would be over, and I'd never know who they were or what they said. "As hostesses it's our duty to help the guests. Maybe there's something we could do."

I slowly opened the window an inch. The voices were definitely female. I recognized Alexia's voice right away because all she ever did was shout, but the other voice took me a moment. *Katrina*, I mouthed the name to Mackenzie who had crawled next to me. She nodded.

Alexia said something too softly for us to hear. Katrina slapped Alexia hard across the cheek. She staggered back in the snow with the force of it. "Stay away from me or else!" Katrina shouted and stormed off.

Alexia cupped her cheek and turned to go. We ducked out of sight in the nick of time, but I'd still glimpsed Alexia's expression. She was smirking. I had no doubt she'd sort of deserved the slap.

"Strange behaviour for two people who just met," I said.

"It didn't take us long to dislike Alexia."

"Katrina started acting strange at the party

yesterday," I reminded Mackenzie.

"Yes, so?"

"What if she started acting weird because she spotted Alexia?"

"If they already know each other, it's a pretty big coincidence to meet here."

"We should keep an eye on those two," I said.

Mackenzie glanced at the clock on the nightstand. "Maybe you should keep an eye on the time. We better hurry or we are going to be late!"

Grandma had bought us these fancy red jumpsuits to wear to the party. She was really playing up the angle that we were cousins. I felt ridiculous in mine. I refused to wear the heart-shaped earrings, but I liked the matching bracelets with the Love Late in Life logo. Mackenzie loved all of it. I allowed her to do my hair. Nothing too girlie, just a complicated braid so I didn't have to worry about my hair for the rest of the day. Once we were dressed, we climbed into our snowsuits, boots and gloves and carried our matching ballet flats.

We were supposed to make sure the guests were awake, deliver the day's agenda, and direct them to the bath house. There was no such thing as ice toilets, thank goodness, so anyone who stayed overnight in an ice room had to shower and get ready in the nearby bath house, which was full of toilets, showers, changing rooms and storage rooms where their luggage was ready and waiting for them.

As we entered the courtyard, I bumped Mackenzie. "Thanks for earlier."

"What?" She bumped me back.

"You know, about my mom."

"Sorry I couldn't find out more."

"Thanks for trying." I knew a bit more about my mom than I did yesterday. Maybe bit by bit I'd piece together the puzzle of my mom. "But no more secrets, OK?" I said.

When we passed the tower of ice with the resort logo, I noticed something was different. Something was frozen in one of the ice blocks. I'd passed it loads of times, and I never remembered seeing that before. As we walked closer, the frozen shape came into focus. But it couldn't be. My mind was playing tricks. Mackenzie was right about my overactive imagination. I was seeing . . . no, wait. I squeezed my eyes shut and then opened them again. But the gruesome image was still there. As we passed the sculpture, I knew what was frozen in the ice with grotesque certainty. It was a severed human finger!

“What’s wrong?” Mackenzie asked when I stopped frozen like one of Sven’s ice sculptures. Then she followed my line of sight and screamed. I covered her mouth with my gloved hand. We didn’t need to alert every guest, staff member, moose and polar bear in a mile radius that there was a massive problem.

She screamed.

And screamed.

And screamed some more.

I tried to pull her away, but our eyes were glued

to the strange sight. "I'm sure there's a reasonable explanation."

"For a-a s-s-severed. . ." she stammered.

Then we heard it. Faint snickers at first and then full-on belly laughs. I gritted my teeth. We'd been pranked.

"Ha! Ha!" Half of TnT sprang from hiding.

"Gotcha again!" The other half pointed his gloved, attached finger at us.

"Oh!" Mackenzie shrieked, still stunned. "You! I should . . . Horrible. Mean."

The adrenaline surge of finding a body part on ice fizzled and was replaced by white-hot anger. "I'm going to kill you," I shouted and lunged at the boys. Mackenzie held me back.

"Now we are even," TnT said in unison.

"We are far from even." I spat the words at them and watched the big goofy grins fade from their lips. "It's your turn to be scared. You better watch out."

"What's going on here?" Mr Ashworth bellowed from the lodge.

TnT bolted like scared rabbits.

"Nothing," I said.

"Sorry," Mackenzie called. Mr Ashworth shrugged and disappeared back inside.

As we walked to the ice hotel, I realized that I was furious that I'd been so easily tricked and admired TnT a bit for such a well-planned prank. "So what should we do to retaliate?"

"I vote for freezing their pants," Mackenzie replied.

"Nice one," I said. "Where did that idea come from? You don't really seem like the prankster type."

"You learn a lot at boarding school," she said with a devious smirk.

"Pickled herring in their boots?"

"Hair-removal cream in their shampoo?"

"That's a bit harsh."

She smiled. "They may be TnT, but we're like. . ."

"The A-bomb."

We traded prank ideas until we reached the ice hotel. All the guests were awake, and we delivered the day's agendas. Our next duty was to help prepare the lodge's main dining hall for lunch and the arrival of the *Melting Your Hearts* competition winners. Ten men and women over sixty-five, and their grandchildren, had won all-expenses-paid trips to the Winter Wonder Resort this weekend. We ditched our snow gear in our room and then headed to the dining hall.

The hall had twinkly heart-shaped lights strung from the ceiling. Red rose petals were scattered everywhere like confetti. Grandma was organizing something on a skirted table by the entrance. Shauna was setting out heart-shaped centrepieces made of red, pink and white roses. Mackenzie nudged me in Grandma's direction. "Perfect time to get some answers."

"She looks busy," I said, suddenly nervous to talk to my own grandma.

"She's always busy," Mackenzie replied. "Go help her out and slip in a few questions. I'll keep everyone out of your way."

"Thanks," I said, but didn't move.

"Go!" She nudged me forward, and I stumbled towards Grandma.

"Good morning, darling." Grandma gave me a quick hug. "Can you finish alphabetizing the nametags?"

"No prob," I said, scattering the bag of nametags on the table. I found my grandma's quickly, because it had a special red border. "Do you want yours now?"

"Thanks." She clipped it on to her expensive silk, rose-print blouse. It was no accident that it matched the colours of the centrepieces exactly.

I had to think of a way for Grandma to tell me my mom's last name, but I couldn't ask directly. Grandma would clam up like she always did, if I asked her point-blank about my mom. "So am I a Sinclair?"

Grandma squinted at me. She did that a lot. I wasn't sure if she didn't understand my American accent or didn't understand me. A little of both probably. "Oh, yes, I guess you are," she said.

"Is that your real last name?"

More squinting.

"You know, were you born Ariadne Sinclair?" I concentrated on moving the nametags around. I was afraid she could read my real motivation in the twitching of my eye.

"Yes, Sinclair is my family name," she said, as she checked the contents of each welcome packet. "I never saw the point of taking any of my husbands' names."

Now we were getting somewhere. "Husbands?" I tried to sound like I was teasing her. This was no big deal. Not a fact-finding mission. Just playful banter between grandmother and granddaughter.

"I've had my fair share," she said.

"What is a fair share?" I asked.

Grandma stopped what she was doing. I'd pushed too hard. I'd blown it. Disappointment stung my insides.

"Four," she said with a laugh. "That's my limit."

"Four," I repeated and remembered what Mackenzie had said about a rock star boyfriend. "Anyone I'd know?"

Her eyes glazed as if a movie of her past loves was playing in the distance. "Liam McDonald, Niall Murphy, and Harry Thompson," she said after a long pause.

I repeated their names in my head. One of them was my grandfather. Then I realized, "That's three."

"Louis Archer," she said with a sigh. "He was my first and one true love."

A weird thing to say after naming three other husbands. "Is Louis Archer my grandfather?"

She squinted at me again. "Yes."

"Could I meet him?"

Tears welled in her eyes. She shook her head. "No, I'm sorry, my darling."

She didn't need to say it. Louis Archer was dead. A gumball-sized lump formed in my throat and prevented me from asking anything else. I was suddenly sad. Sad that Grandma had lost her one true love and sad that I'd never meet my grandpa.

She cocked her head and studied me. One solitary tear escaped down her cheek. "He would have liked you," she whispered. "He would have liked you a lot." Grandma cleared her throat and wiped her eyes. "I better check in with the chef."

I felt terrible that I'd made Grandma cry. I didn't mean to. I wondered if Grandma realized she'd given me a vital clue about my mom. Beatrice Archer. Now I knew her full name.

We'd only checked in half of the *Melting Your Hearts* guests and my cheeks already ached from smiling. The pensioners received their nametags, and we helped them download the app. Adriane and Shauna wanted to show the VIPs how the app would work. While the grandkids had a separate itinerary that included visiting the ice maze, sledding, skating and skiing, the old folks were treated to speed-dating the Love Late in Life way. I couldn't wait to ditch the old folks and have some fun outdoors.

"Help yourself to the buffet," Mackenzie said, her smile never faltered even though she'd said it a million times already. "The programme will start in a few minutes."

I ducked behind Mackenzie. "Don't look now but it's your BFF Alexia," I whispered. I'd be happy never to see that drama queen again.

Alexia pushed to the front of the line.

"Good afternoon, Alexia," Mackenzie said. "Here's your nametag."

"How's your grandmother?" I asked, poking at a sore spot.

"Fine, I guess," she said as if it didn't matter. "She texted me late last night. How absolutely rude to leave me like that. Is she here?"

"No, not yet," I said. "She's probably still enjoying the peace and quiet."

Mackenzie elbowed me in the ribs. "Is that Michael Kors?" Mackenzie indicated Alexia's oversized pink handbag.

"It's so last season, but I didn't want to bring anything good to this place." Her tone was sour.

"Help yourself to the buffet," Mackenzie said, her tone twice as bouncy as before.

"Buffet? Seriously?" Alexia moaned.

I edged around Mackenzie ready to give this brat

a piece of my mind, but Mackenzie blocked me.

"I'm absolutely ravenous. Haven't had a decent thing to eat since I arrived in this God-forsaken place. Can you tell me what's on the buffet? I have allergies and need to be ever-so careful. I hope the chef has been apprised of my dietary restrictions."

Mackenzie showed Alexia her lunch ticket. "It clearly notes that you are allergic to shellfish. The kitchen has been instructed, and no shellfish is on the menu."

Alexia pinched the edges of her ticket as if it was covered in goo and sauntered off to have her lunch. Shauna and the chef were arranging the serving dishes on the buffet. Katrina was filling her plate. I remembered Alexia and Katrina's fight this morning. This could get interesting. While Mackenzie checked in the next few guests, I watched Alexia. She was like the token mean girl on every reality show that you loved to hate and had to watch.

"I've lost my appetite," Katrina said and handed the plate to Shauna.

Alexia marched right over and snatched the plate out of Shauna's hand. "Some people are so wasteful," Alexia said, loud enough for the entire room to hear. "They throw away something that's perfectly satisfactory. Not just food, people too."

Everyone stared at Alexia and Katrina.

"You should know," Katrina replied and walked as far away from Alexia as she could.

The show was over. I returned to work.

"I'm David Johnson." A silver-haired man walked over to the registration table. He was handsome for a grandpa with dimples that made him seem boyish.

"Welcome!" Mackenzie gave her *Melting Your Hearts* speech.

"This is my grandson, Blake," the man said, gesturing to the empty space beside him. He spun around, searching for his missing grandson. "He was just here."

I handed him the last two nametags.

"It's the strangest thing," Mr Johnson continued.

"I'm sure he'll be back soon," I said, trying to help.

"No, not that," the man continued. "I don't remember entering this competition. I've never won anything before."

"Congratulations," Mackenzie said with her perkiness in overdrive. "I hope you and your grandson have a lovely time."

"Is that your grandson?" I asked when I spotted a guy with the same dimples peeking from behind the human-sized ice sculpture of the Love Late in Life logo that was near the door to the dining hall.

"There you are," Mr Johnson said and waved his grandson over. Blake darted from his hiding place and stood in his grandpa's shadow. "This is . . . I didn't get your names."

"I'm Chase and this is my cousin Berkeley," I piped up afraid that Mackenzie would be too distracted by a cute boy to remember her cover story.

"Hi," Mackenzie said in a soft sing-song voice. She twisted on her tiptoes.

Argh! Was she flirting again? "The buffet is over

there. Help yourself." I handed them their lunch tickets.

"I'm not really hungry." Blake turned to go.

"We've been travelling for ages," Mr Johnson said. "You need to eat."

Blake followed his grandpa to the buffet. "Don't you think it's weird how he hides behind his grandpa?" I whispered to Mackenzie.

"I think he's cute," she murmured. She couldn't take her eyes off him. Love early in life.

"Let's eat!" I looped my arm through Mackenzie's.

"The itinerary says we are stationed at the registration table until—"

"Everyone has checked in, and I'm hungry," I said, but Mackenzie didn't budge. "Ariadne and Shauna want us to keep up our strength. And look: there's a whole table of desserts." That's all it took. We were on the move.

Alexia, who was posed like a model in the middle of the room, stopped us as we passed. "Girls, this food tastes absolutely diabolical." She sneered and poked a cheese puff with a celery stick.

"We're off duty," I said. "Tell someone who cares." She'd complain about anything. Her diamonds were probably too sparkly and her boyfriend too handsome and her mansion simply too big.

"Sorry," Mackenzie apologised on my behalf. "I'll tell the chef," she called to Alexia as I dragged her towards the buffet.

"You!" Alexia shrieked. I shouldn't have insulted her, but she was a total diva. I cringed and waited for an Alexia explosion until I realized that she was staring at someone behind me. Her face scrunched in confusion. "What are you..." She began to cough. Not like a dainty cough either but a full-on, smoker's hacking cough.

Her plate toppled out of her hand and crashed to the floor. Then as if in slow motion, she staggered left and then right. She was wheezing and gasping for air. She collapsed on to a table, clawing a fistful of roses from the centrepiece as she slid to the floor. A broken mannequin in a puddle of petals.

8

“Everyone back up,” Shauna shouted as she rushed to Alexia, diving for her like a baseball player stealing home base.

Mackenzie grabbed my arm, accidentally digging her sparkly red nails into me. “I don’t think she’s breathing,” she whispered as if a loud voice might make it true. Shauna was moving Alexia into the recovery position.

“No, she’s fine,” I reassured Mackenzie, but I was far from sure of that. Exclamation marks were pinging in my brain, trying to tell me something, but all I could do was look on in horror.

"Call an ambulance," Shauna yelled at Grandma when she broke through the crowd.

Grandma already had her cell phone in her hand. "What's the number? What do I call?"

"One-one-two!" someone with a Swedish accent responded.

"I've already called an ambulance," Mr Ashworth yelled from somewhere. "I'll get the first aid kit. Ariadne, alert security and the front desk." Grandma muscled through the crowd towards the front door.

I wasn't sure that Band-Aids and aspirin were going to help Alexia. Something was really wrong. Shauna brushed a stray curl away from Alexia's face and whispered into Alexia's ear, probably telling her not to worry. Alexia had landed on and broken her plate. Two red streaks coloured her cheek. Food was smeared all over and around her.

The panicked fog cleared from my brain. That was it. The food. Alexia's allergies. "Berkeley, find Alexia's handbag."

We brushed back the crowd, scanning the floor for a pink handbag. "Got it!" Mackenzie held it up.

"Here!" I raised my hands to catch it. I dumped the contents on the floor. "EpiPen," I told Mackenzie as we fell to our hands and knees and searched through the mountain of make-up, loose change, phone, perfume, but no EpiPen.

She had to have one. Someone with a serious food allergy always carried an EpiPen. I fumbled with the handbag, feeling in every pocket and compartment. Finally, "I got it!"

I lurched for Alexia with the EpiPen in hand. I'd taken a first aid class, and a girl in my elementary school had multiple allergies. I'd watched her use an EpiPen once after a parent brought in peanut butter cookies. "Let me through," I told Shauna who was protectively curled around Alexia.

I formed a fist around the EpiPen and pulled off the safety cap. I must have looked like a serial killer ready to strike as I raised the injector.

"What are you doing?" Shauna shouted and batted me away.

"Alexia has food allergies. This could be anaphylactic shock," I said. If it was a food allergy, I had to act quickly or Alexia could die.

"Chase, back away." Shauna shoved me in the chest.

"Help me," I begged Mackenzie and nodded in Shauna's direction. "Trust me." Mackenzie did as I asked, wrapped her arms around Shauna and pulled her away.

I placed the black tip of the EpiPen against Alexia's leg, rammed the injector against her thigh and removed it again.

Alexia's body convulsed. In that second I felt as if my heart stopped beating. My body flushed cold with fear.

"What have you done?" Shauna screamed and broke free from Mackenzie. She knocked me away with the full force of her body. I tumbled backwards but kept my eyes glued to Alexia.

Then Alexia gasped.

Shauna burst into tears. She must have been as relieved as I was.

Alexia was still struggling to breathe. I crawled over to her. "You are going to be OK," I told Alexia. "I used your EpiPen."

Her breath steadied into shallow gasps. Her skin was pale. All the fire and fight from earlier had drained away.

"Just breathe," I told her. I noticed a huge bump on her head from where she'd bashed it as she fell. She had been nothing but horrible from the millisecond she arrived, but I wouldn't wish this on anyone. I hoped she'd be OK. I prayed I'd done the right thing.

Suddenly Grandma was at my side. "How is she?" she asked.

"She's breathing." I explained about Alexia's allergies and what I'd done. Mackenzie and Shauna joined us and formed a protective circle around Alexia.

Shauna had stopped crying, but her face was still red and blotchy. "Your quick response may have saved Alexia's life. I don't know how this could have happened," she muttered.

"We'll worry about that later," Grandma told her. "The important thing is that she'll recover."

How did it happen? I'd heard Shauna instruct the chef myself last week. I'd seen Alexia's lunch ticket. Two accidents in two days. Not small *oops!* moments but accidents that could have been deadly. Maybe they weren't accidents.

Grandma and Shauna would take it from here. Mackenzie must have been thinking the same thing. We retreated and found a quiet place at the back of the room. "Now do you believe me?" I whispered to Mackenzie. "Something weird is definitely going on here."

Mackenzie nodded. "Look," she said and gestured to Katrina, who was whispering something to Blake. "Katrina seems to know everyone."

"In crises, sometimes..." I started but then Katrina hugged Blake. He kissed her forehead. Those weren't the actions of complete strangers.

"Can I have everyone's attention?" Shauna was completely calm and in control again. She asked everyone to follow her into the lobby.

"Let's go," I said to Mackenzie and headed in the opposite direction to Shauna.

"Where are you going?" Mackenzie asked and picked up a jumbo chocolate cookie from the buffet table as we passed. She took a huge bite.

"I think Alexia was intentionally poisoned," I said.

Mackenzie spat the cookie into her hand. "What?" She studied the cookie as if the hunks of chocolate were arsenic. "That's a bit dramatic." She placed what remained of the cookie on a discarded plate.

We kept moving. "The girl had to have enemies." I punched open the swinging doors that lead to the kitchen. "We were on the sled that was meant for Alexia and her grandma yesterday. It could have been sabotaged. Today Alexia collapses. That can't be an accident."

The chef and his dozen or so kitchen staff were huddled together. They already knew about Alexia. The platters that had been so artfully arranged with cheeses, meats and breads were scattered on the long stainless steel prep tables. Something was smoking on the stovetop. The tart smell of burning food sizzled in the room.

"What are we doing in here?" Mackenzie asked. "How can you think of food at a time like this?"

The room hushed as the faint sound of a siren swelled in the distance. The ambulance was coming for Alexia. The kitchen staff seemed to wake and stir again. The chef barked orders and everyone scattered. I thought they looked like actors in my high school play; not the lead characters, but the ones in the chorus who tried to look like they knew what they were doing. The kitchen workers didn't know how to act when one of their guests laid on the dining room floor probably as the result of their cooking.

"I'm not hungry," I said to Mackenzie, but I did have food on my mind.

"Then what are we doing in here?" she asked.

"Looking for the murder weapon."

9

"You shouldn't be in here."

I flinched at the sharpness of his voice. The white chef's hat looked out of place on his head, like a cherry on top of a watermelon.

Mackenzie was already inching back towards the dining room door. "Maybe we should go."

"Um, Frank. . ." I started.

"It's Frans," Mackenzie corrected. Foreign names never seemed to stick in my brain.

"Hi, Frans, could I ask you a few questions?"

He glared at us.

"I'm Chase and this is Berkeley." I gave him my friendliest smile but my lips wouldn't cooperate. He was making me feel so uncomfortable. "We are Ariadne Sinclair's granddaughters."

"Ah, Ariadne." He softened. "Lovely lady."

How could I ask if he accidentally poisoned someone? "I loved the meatballs you served today."

"They are my speciality," he said. Was that almost a smile?

"I guess you heard what happened in there." I nodded to the dining room.

"Ja." He was stony-faced and glaring again.

"Just checking. . ." This was the tricky part. "There wasn't any seafood on the buffet."

He slammed his hand on the stainless steel table in front of him, setting the kitchen's metal pots, pans and utensils clattering. "Are they blaming this on me?" he roared. "No shellfish at all. I carefully reviewed the dietary restrictions of our guests."

"It could have been an accident?" I tried. "Maybe one of the kitchen staff—"

"My kitchen is clean. My staff are professionals. We know how serious food allergies can be."

"You can't be one hundred per cent sure," Mackenzie added. "Maybe—"

I cringed as Frans interrupted. "Are you calling me a liar?" he shouted and everyone in the kitchen froze. "Get out! Now! This is not my fault!" His eyes were practically bulging out of his head.

"Way to go," I mumbled to Mackenzie as we headed for the back door.

"What?" she said. Sometimes she understood facts and figures better than people. "I was trying to help."

"Here!" I removed two parkas from the pegs near the back door of the kitchen. I handed one to Mackenzie and took the other one for myself. I winced as I zipped it up. The coats were for the kitchen staff, and they smelled like the grossest soup on the planet: raw meat and onions and body odour.

Mackenzie held the dirty coat at arm's length between pinched fingers. "No, thanks," she paused, maybe realizing that the resort's dumpsters were lined up outside that door. "Why are we going outside anyway?"

"Looking for clues," I told her. I'd watched enough murder mysteries with my dad to know you had to search for clues fast.

"You're not Sherlock, and I'm no Watson." She tried to hang up the coat, but I blocked her.

I didn't have time to argue. "Are you coming or not?" I marched outside. The cold hit me with a hard slap. I pulled up the hood on the parka and found gloves in the pockets, but the bottom half of my body was stinging from the freezing wind.

Mackenzie stomped up behind me. She huffed with every step. Her parka was zipped so only her eyes were visible. She'd tied another parka around her waist and put gloves on her hands and feet.

"Start looking," I said.

"For what?"

"I don't know. Fish something." I didn't have a plan really.

"You think someone put shellfish something in Alexia's food."

I nodded.

"You think whoever it was would want to dispose of the evidence as quickly as possible and then return to the dining room before anyone noticed they were missing."

No, I hadn't thought it through like that, but I replied, "Yes, exactly."

"Then it stands to reason that they'd throw it in the dumpster nearest the door. . ." Her voice trailed off. "Oh, no." She shook her head so fiercely that her hood flew off. "I am not searching that dumpster. Can't you smell it from here?"

"You're imagining things," I said, and flipped open the lid to the first dumpster. "Everything would freeze quickly out here so it won't be so bad." I laced my gloved fingers together. "I'll boost you up. Just look inside."

"I'll boost you up."

"You're taller, and I'm stronger."

"You owe me," she said as she stepped her gloved

foot in my hand. I wished I'd thought of that. My toes were already numb in my red ballet shoes. I hoisted her higher. She shrieked and clutched the side of the dumpster.

"See anything?" I tried to stand still but the cold and her weight were making me wobbly.

"Lots of . . . yuck!"

"What is it?"

"You don't want to know." She lifted herself up.

"Get on my shoulders," I told her and she shifted so she was sitting on my shoulders. I held on to the handle on the dumpster to steady us.

"Wait, I see something." She lunged forward, taking me with her.

My body banged against the dumpster. "Hey, watch it!"

That's when I heard it. Laughter. TnT.

"Argh!" I jerked around, forgetting that Mackenzie was balanced on my shoulders.

"AAAHHH!" she echoed as she slid down my back, and we tumbled to the ground. I heard something clank on the frozen ground and clatter as it rolled away.

"Looks like they've thrown away two perfectly good girls," one T said to the other.

"What use are girls anyway?" the other said, and they burst out laughing.

Mackenzie clutched at my coat as she tried to stand, but her gloved feet and my stupid shoes slid on the ice, and we crashed to the ground again. At least the heat of my embarrassment was warming me.

"Let us help," TnT said, and each extended us a hand.

I batted it away, but Mackenzie accepted the help. I flipped to all fours and clawed my way up the dumpster.

"Looking for this?" one of the boys said as he picked up a small plastic vial and handed it to Mackenzie, who gave it to me.

I read the label and my gut clenched in worry. "You guys didn't sprinkle that on the buffet to prank us."

"What?" one said. "No!" the other exclaimed. "Berkeley threw it at us."

"You found that in the dumpster?" I asked Mackenzie. She nodded. It was a vial of dried fish flakes. Someone could have easily sprinkled this over the buffet or Alexia's plate. She said the food had tasted bad. "Are there fish tanks in the resort?" I asked TnT.

"This is not exactly the right environment for fish," Left Twin said.

"Yeah, they don't serve sushi popsicles," Right Twin added, and they busted out laughing again.

"It's not funny," I said, remembering Alexia curled on the floor, struggling to breathe.

They stopped laughing. "Wait, does this have something to do with what happened to that girl?" Right Twin asked.

"She was allergic to shellfish and look at the ingredients." I held out the vial so they could read the list of ingredients, which included shellfish.

"There's no other logical reason someone would have this here, is there?" Mackenzie asked.

"Come on," Left Twin said. "You think someone intentionally poisoned her?" The boys started to laugh but stopped mid-smirk when they saw we were serious.

The kitchen door slammed open. TnT bolted. It made me want to run too, but my feet were so cold I wasn't sure I could walk. I don't know why, but I instinctively stuffed the vial of fish food in the pocket of the parka.

Mr Ashworth peered outside. "There you are," he said to us but watched the boys skirt around the building and disappear. "Ariadne wants everyone in the lobby for an announcement." He held open the door for us, and we followed him inside.

We replaced the parkas. Before I removed my gloves, I found a plastic bag and wrapped the vial inside – like those crime scene investigators did on TV. I slipped the vial into the pocket of my jumpsuit and returned the gloves.

When Mackenzie noticed what I was doing, she whispered, "Good thinking. There might be fingerprints."

We made our way with the other guests to the lobby. I jumped when I heard sirens. They quickly faded into the distance, taking Alexia away. I didn't like the feel of the vial in my pocket. It was evidence, and it made me feel guilty.

"That's everyone," Mr Ashworth called to Grandma who was standing on a chair in the middle of the lobby.

"Thank you for your patience and cooperation," she said. "Alexia has been taken to the local hospital where we believe she will make a full recovery." She scanned the room as she spoke. "It was a terrible accident. They are trying to contact her grandmother. I'm sure this has been upsetting. Please see Shauna for keys to your rooms in the lodge if you'd like to rest."

Shauna helped Grandma down and then took her place. "If you'd like a diversion, the ice maze is open. Sven will be giving an ice sculpture demonstration in the lobby of the ice hotel in approximately thirty minutes. I hope you won't let this . . . unfortunate incident . . . spoil your time with us."

Mackenzie and I looked at each other. It wasn't just me then. She thought that was a strange thing to say too. Alexia had almost died. OK, she wasn't very nice. Everyone in the dining room had heard her bratty outbursts, but how could anyone see what happened to Alexia and not feel bad?

One hand shot up near the front of the crowd.

"I'd like to leave," a male voice said.

"That's Blake," Mackenzie whispered to me. Today had sucked, but why was he so anxious to leave?

Shauna stuttered and stammered.

"I'm very sorry for the upsetting day, but there's no reason to leave," Grandma said. She was so calm, so in control. I admired that. "The paramedics told me that a blizzard is on its way. The airport and train stations are being closed. He urged us to remain here for the time being. . ."

Grandma continued to answer questions and reassure everyone that everything was hunky-dory. I wanted to believe her, but I shivered with an imagined chill. We were stranded here with someone who had deliberately hurt Alexia.

10

"You've got to tell her," Mackenzie said, scooting me towards the crowd surrounding my grandma. Some of the older guests had left for their rooms. Most of the younger guests were heading to the ice maze. Blake and Katrina left out the front door together.

"I'll tell Grandma later in private," I said, digging my heels in.

"Tell Ariadne what?" Shauna appeared next to us, clipboard in hand.

"Nothing," I said. I wasn't ready to tell anyone

about my suspicions yet. All I really had was a vial of fish food and a gut feeling. I didn't want to upset Grandma and Shauna unless I was abso-freaking-lutely sure.

"I need your help," Shauna said. "This Alexia thing has wreaked havoc with my schedule. Change into your snowsuits and set up Sven's demonstration in the ice hotel lobby." She handed us a sheet from her clipboard. "This details everything you need to do. I've ask reception to call Sven. He should be there soon."

"Will do," I said, happy for the distraction.

"What about..." Mackenzie started.

"We've got work to do," I interrupted and led the way to our room. "I promise I'll tell Grandma later," I said to Mackenzie once we were safely in our room. "We need more proof before we make such a wild and crazy accusation." We quickly changed into our snow gear. I tucked the vial of fish food in the pocket of my snowsuit.

The atmosphere had changed. I could feel it as we trudged to the ice hotel. The snow was falling heavily. We could barely see a few feet in front of us. We huddled together to battle the wind, but it was more than the weather. Everyone and everything felt on edge. Mackenzie twitched at every sound. I wondered what or who might be lurking nearby. Was someone plotting another "accident"?

The ice hotel lobby was empty, which made the space seem colder. Mackenzie called out the to-dos from Shauna's list and soon the lobby was ready for Sven. A huge block of ice, taller than Mackenzie and as wide as the two of us side by side, had been placed in the centre of the lobby. Sven would transform the big ice cube into something amazing right before our eyes. I'd seen him do it before.

"Where's Sven?" Mackenzie asked with a worried look on her face. People were arriving.

"Maybe I should go look for him?"

Mackenzie grabbed my arm. "Don't leave me."

Just then we heard the *clink* and *clack* of Sven's tools as he jogged through the main corridor. Mackenzie and I met him at the table we'd set up for his demonstration. Sweat dotted his forehead. "C-can you help me get organized?" he asked as he lobbed a big tool case on the table. His hands were shaking.

"Are you OK?" I asked.

"Ja, ja," he said but didn't look at us. He concentrated on laying out his equipment.

Was he upset about Alexia? I doubted it. He probably hadn't met her. Did he know what happened?

Sven prepared his chainsaw while Mackenzie and I positioned the chisels and other sharp blades that he used to shave the ice. More and more people arrived.

"Do you want some water or a cup of tea?" Mackenzie asked Sven when everything was in place.

He shook his head. "I am ready."

I clapped my hands. "Can I have your attention please?" The room was packed with snow-suited figures. I introduced Sven and he got right to work. His chainsaw roared to life. He cut away large chunks of ice.

"What's he making?" I whispered to Mackenzie.

Mackenzie consulted her checklist. "Says here he's supposed to be carving Cupid."

I cringed at the lameness.

"I know, right?" Mackenzie groaned.

We cocked our heads and tried to see Cupid emerging from the ice. I could see a heart taking shape.

My body was twitching to move. "Sven's got everything under control," I whispered to Mackenzie. "I think we should check in at the ice maze and make sure no one's lost in that one tricky dead end with the howling wolf ice sculpture."

Mackenzie nodded. She knew I wasn't concerned about our guests. I wanted to investigate, find more clues and prove to Grandma and Shauna that something deadly was going on here.

Sven's audience blocked the front door. "We'll have to go out the back." We slowly edged around the room and slipped down the main corridor and wound our way through the hotel. The hum of voices and the rattle of Sven's tools faded the further we moved into the hotel.

Mackenzie gasped and hugged me close. "Did you see that?" she whispered.

"What?" I jerked free and spun in a slow circle. Panic electrified my body. I didn't see anything.

"I thought I saw something move over there." She pointed down the corridor a few feet away. "A reflection or something."

I inched forward and to check it out. Up ahead the shadows seemed to shift in the ice. I darted back to Mackenzie.

"W-what i-is it?" she stammered.

"I didn't see anyone," I said, which was true but didn't feel like the whole story. I didn't need Mackenzie freaking out on me. "We are jumpy after, you know, what happened. I've got you imagining things," I said with a fake laugh. "We'll feel better once we're outside."

We turned the corner and stopped dead in our tracks. "You saw it this time, right?" Mackenzie asked. I nodded. The shadows had returned.

"It's probably a trick of the light." I took a step forward.

Mackenzie stopped me. "I bet it's TnT."

TnT, of course. How could I have been so stupid? I wasn't going to let them trick me again. "In here," I told Mackenzie and slipped into the next room we passed. "It's our turn to scare them." I looked around for inspiration. On the far side of the room was a sculpture of a bird's nest with a load of ice eggs. The largest egg in the middle looked as if it was cracking and a tiny beak was emerging. Sven's sculptures always had these little fun touches. "Grab a few of those eggs," I told Mackenzie. "Just the small ones around the edge."

"We shouldn't wreck Sven's sculpture," she said, but did it anyway.

"We'll put them back," I said, taking the ice eggs from her. "I'll roll one in the hall to attract their attention, and then another. We'll hide and when they investigate, we'll pounce on them."

"I don't know. . ."

"All you have to do is hide," I told her and rolled one egg into the hallway. I dived behind the bird's nest. Mackenzie flicked on her phone and looked around for someplace to hide. There weren't many options; just three blocks of ice – a big one with a reindeer pelt for the bed, a smaller one that was the table and the third which was a chair. "Come on. You're going to ruin it." I chucked another egg out of the door. It hit the icy floor with a *splat*.

Mackenzie dived under the reindeer pelt. The light of her phone flickered again. But instead of hiding quietly, she screamed and leaped from the bed, taking the reindeer pelt with her. It wasn't her normal girly yelp when she saw a spider. This was the kind of scream that made my insides jiggle like jelly.

"What is it? What's the matter?" I was at her side.

Her face was as white as a marshmallow. She pointed to the bed and then crumpled into the ice chair.

What had scared her? I needed to know, but part of me didn't want to find out. I took a deep breath. It was probably nothing. She'd spooked herself. I took another step. Maybe it was another of TnT's rubber finger pranks. I took a step closer. Yeah, that was probably it. I switched on my phone and directed the light to the bed.

I stifled a gasp. It looked like a body was frozen in the ice, but that couldn't be. My phone light faded. That was ridiculous. I wasn't going to let TnT fool me again. They could have put something in the ice bed, like they did the block of ice in the courtyard. It was probably a mannequin. I looked behind me expecting to find the snickering pair peeking around the doorway. The corridor seemed darker than it had a few minutes ago.

"Is it. . ." Mackenzie blubbered. "It is, isn't it?"

I stepped right next to the bed and leaned over. I slowly swept the light from my phone from the foot of the bed to the head.

I screamed and backed away, landing on Mackenzie and then falling hard on to the floor. My phone skidded across the room.

It was definitely not a mannequin. That was a body. A dead body was trapped inside the ice.

"Is it?" Mackenzie asked again.

I nodded. My brain and body were frozen in fear. I knew it was a real body because I recognized the face. "It's Lucinda Sterling."

I scrambled for my phone as we staggered out of the room and towards the exit. We stumbled into the cold on wobbly legs, holding our phones in the air searching for a signal. The snow was coming down so heavily we could only see the faint glow of the lights that lead to the lodge.

"What do we dial for emergencies?" I couldn't remember what they'd told us earlier when Alexia needed an ambulance.

"One-one-two," Mackenzie said.

I pulled off my gloves and dialled. "Hello, police," I said when someone answered. "Emergency." I remembered the phrase Shauna had taught me. "Jag talar inte Svenska." I know I messed up the pronunciation, but I hoped the operator understood that I didn't speak Swedish.

"What is your emergency?" The man's voice was calm and reassuring.

"Dead body. Dead body." I couldn't think of

what else to say.

"Calm down and tell me what happened," the man said. "Are you saying that you've found a dead body?"

I nodded, in my panic forgetting that they couldn't see my head bobbing in agreement.

Mackenzie took the phone from me. Her hands were shaking. She took a deep breath. "We are at the Winter Wonder Resort." Another huge breath. "There's a dead body frozen in one of the ice beds." I had to hand it to her. She wasn't Miss Action-Adventure, but she could pull it together when she needed to. If she could suck it up and be brave-ish, I could too. I shook off the shock.

She listened and nodded. "Lucinda Sterling." She paused and nodded some more. "No, but we will do that right now." Another pause. "I see. Are you sure?" Another pause. "Yes, I understand." She hung up and handed the phone to me.

"Shouldn't we stay on the line until they arrive?" I was speaking fast and tripping over my words. "Should we block off the crime scene?"

"The police aren't coming."

"That's not funny."

"I'm not joking. The roads are closed. They will arrive as soon as they can, but it could be more than twenty-four hours. They are a small police station, and the snow storm has already caused several accidents. We are supposed to alert the resort's security and let them handle it until the police can arrive."

"Right," I said as fear surged through me again. I'd been in worse situations before. "We saved the day in the Maldives, and we can do it again," I said, faking a load of confidence. *Fake it until you make it*, Dad used to tell me. Pretend to be brave and eventually you will feel brave.

"I don't want to do it again," Mackenzie whispered.

"We don't have a choice," I told her. "If we can survive a heist, vicious eels, a bomb, man-eating sharks and a kidnapping, we can handle one little old dead body."

"The dead body's not the problem," Mackenzie said, looking over her shoulder. "It's the killer."

11

"And there's one more thing." Mackenzie took a deep breath. She had reported everything to Grandma and Shauna. They were our next calls after the police. We'd met them outside the room with Lucinda's dead body on ice. They'd seen the body. Mackenzie and I stayed outside the room until they returned. Mackenzie nudged me. "Show them."

I showed them the vial of fish food, still wrapped in the plastic bag to preserve evidence.

"What is it?" Shauna took it from me and

removed it from the plastic before I could stop her.

"Is that fish food?" Grandma asked, taking the vial from Shauna. If there were any incriminating fingerprints, they were ruined now.

I nodded. "We found it in the dumpster behind the lodge."

"I'm not going to ask why or how you were searching a dumpster," Grandma said.

I wasn't going to explain. I had a feeling it would only get me in trouble. "Alexia is allergic to shellfish. There are no aquariums at the Winter Wonder Resort—"

"You think someone used this to poison Alexia," Grandma interrupted.

"I also think that our dogsled accident wasn't an accident," I said. "Someone was trying to kill the Sterlings."

Grandma's face matched the snow. Her eyes searched mine. She was speechless and that scared me more than finding the dead body.

"What do you want us to do, Grandma?" I asked. She stared at me.

"Should we assemble the guests and let them know what happened?" Mackenzie suggested.

"No!" Shauna blurted. "Maybe there's a reasonable explanation for this."

Seriously? Even my wacky imagination couldn't think of any non-scary explanation for how someone ends up dead in a block of ice.

"I think Mackenzie is right." Grandma stood straighter, back in control. "We should—"

"We don't want to create a panic," Shauna interrupted. "We'll rope off this area and have the resort's security team stand guard. For now, we tell no one."

Grandma squinted at Shauna. "I'm not sure—"

"What good will it do to scare everyone?" Shauna asked, drowning out Grandma's concern. "We will lose control of the situation. We want everyone to stay calm, right?"

Grandma nodded, but I could tell from her wrinkled forehead that she wasn't completely convinced.

"I'll put this in a safety deposit box in reception."

Shauna shoved the fish food in her messenger bag. "I'll give it to the police as soon as they arrive."

"Create and post a few signs to keep people away from the ice hotel for now," Grandma told Shauna. "We'll adjust the itinerary to keep everyone in the lodge tonight. We can use the weather as our excuse."

Shauna rushed away. Maybe she was hiding it well, but she didn't seem that upset.

I was trying not to completely lose it, but there was a dead body in a block of ice right behind me. A dead body. In ice. It didn't seem like a real thing that could happen. I was going to have to use my wildest imagination to block that image from my mind.

The two resort security guards raced over. "Body? Where?"

We pointed to the room behind us. Grandma barked orders at them. "Block off this room. Cover the body." The security guards were like something from a police comedy. They were bumbling around and messing up any evidence that might have been in the room.

"These guys don't know what they are doing," I whispered to Mackenzie. "They will never catch who did this."

"That's not their job," Mackenzie said. "They are going to guard the crime scene. That's all."

"Then we are going to have to figure out what happened and why."

She shuddered. "I was afraid you were going to say that."

To say the rest of the night was weird would be like saying Superman was simply an ordinary guy in a tight suit. We helped Grandma and Shauna keep everyone happy and completely unaware that one of their fellow guests was a human ice cube. I watched everyone closely. I was sure that I'd be able to see the guilt in the eyes of whoever did this. I mean you can't just kill someone and then resume your life as usual, but everyone acted no more or less strange than they had before. I found it unnerving that someone had died and yet nothing had changed. Shauna eventually asked me to stop staring at the guests because it was freaking everyone out.

Mackenzie and I couldn't wait until our hostess/ lying-our-butts-off duties were done for the night, and we could escape to our room. Mackenzie wanted to go to bed and pretend that Alexia hadn't been poisoned and Lucinda wasn't dead, but I had a better idea.

I fired up Mackenzie's computer and collapsed on the couch. "What are we doing?" Mackenzie asked as she typed in her password and plopped down next to me.

"Let's find out everything we can about Lucinda and Alexia Sterling," I said and handed the computer to Mackenzie. I was definitely rubbing off on her because she got right to work.

Her search found several web pages. We started reading and clicking links and reading some more. Lucinda Sterling was the retired headmistress of Ingenium International College, an elite boarding school in England. Every article and reference was about how brilliant she was, how amazing the school was or how much she'd done for this charity or that student. She was squeaky clean. We couldn't find one bad word ever uttered about her – except she was a tough headmistress who expected and received the most from her students.

Her granddaughter was the exact opposite.

"Can you check out Alexia's social media stuff?" I asked Mackenzie. A few clicks and taps, and we were in. Alexia had posted a picture of herself almost every day, pouting her lips and staring into the camera. *Gack!* She'd also posted unflattering pictures of other people from celebrities to girls at Ingenium and made nasty comments about them.

"What a witch," Mackenzie muttered.

"I'm surprised it's taken this long for someone to try and off her." I pointed to a particularly nasty comment slamming her teachers at Ingenium.

"Did you read the most recent posts?" Mackenzie asked. "She was kicked out of her uni, and reading between the lines, I think her parents sent her to live with her grandmother in hopes she could rehabilitate her."

"That explains her nasty mood."

"Or maybe she's always like that."

"Check out her profile," I said when I'd seen enough glamour-gross shots of Alexia.

"She is the only child of two very wealthy people," Mackenzie said, scrolling through Alexia's profile. "Look at her address. Doesn't get any posher than that."

"I'm sure there are loads of people who would like to kill Alexia," I said. "But not literally kill her, if you know what I mean."

We climbed into our beds, but Mackenzie kept searching. We eventually fell asleep. I woke at 6:34 a.m. according to my watch. Mackenzie was already tapping away on her laptop.

"Look at this," Mackenzie said as soon as she realized I was awake.

I crawled into bed next to her. I rubbed my eyes and studied her computer screen. "Is that?"

"I think so," Mackenzie said. The photo was of a younger Alexia and Blake.

"How did you find that?" I asked. "I didn't see

any pictures of Blake on Alexia's social media pages." She started speaking computer-geek speak.
"In normal people language," I interrupted.

"I dug around a bit and found posts and pictures Alexia deleted a few years ago. Nothing is ever really deleted. Never forget that."

My dad wouldn't let me on any social media. I needed to remember to thank him. No one could stalk me like we were stalking Alexia.

"It appears that Blake and Alexia dated at Ingenium. A real *It* couple." She showed me a few pictures. They were dressed for a dance and on a yacht somewhere with crystal blue water that reminded me of the Maldives.

Then I remember what Alexia said right before she collapsed. "I think Alexia spotted Blake right before she hit the floor."

"Blake acted weird from the moment he arrived," Mackenzie added. "You remember how he kept hiding behind his grandfather? Also he wanted to leave right after Alexia's accident."

"Blake Johnson." I clicked on a picture of him

and enlarged it so it filled the screen. "Suspect number one."

"Dating her makes him an idiot, not a killer."

"We knew her for all of a day, and we wanted to kill her."

Mackenzie looked at me with disgust. "Not a great choice of words."

"I don't mean for real. You know what I mean. It can't be an accident that Alexia's ex-boyfriend arrives and the next minute she's poisoned."

Mackenzie checked the shared folder where Shauna kept the plans for the launch. "His room is only a few doors away."

"Mackenzie, I'm shocked," I said, rummaging around in my suitcase for something to wear. "You aren't suggesting we go and ask him a few questions."

Mackenzie wasn't moving from her spot covered up in bed. "No, that is not what I am suggesting."

I dressed in jeans and the Winter Wonder Resort sweatshirt Grandma had bought me. I tossed Mackenzie the pair of jeans she'd left draped over the blue leather chair in the corner of the room and the pink sweatshirt with the small designer logo on the front that was piled near her bed.

"Did you hear that?" I said. It sounded like a door opening. "Someone's in the hall."

"You're making that up," she said, but she was out of bed and dressing.

"I'm not joking." I opened the door and poked my head out.

Blake was walking away dressed in his snowsuit.

"It's Blake," I whispered to Mackenzie. "Hurry up or we'll lose him."

"I don't want to catch him," Mackenzie said.

He ducked around the corner, heading towards reception. "What is he doing skulking around at this hour?" I said, grabbing my boots. I needed to know what he was up to.

"What are we doing skulking around at this hour?" she asked.

"We're not skulking, we're following."

"I'm not sure it's smart to be following."

"We'll stay hidden. He won't even know we're here. What can it hurt?"

Mackenzie stopped midway through pulling on her snowsuit. "Seriously?"

OK. That was a stupid thing to say. In these circumstances, it could hurt a lot – like, dead hurt, but I couldn't sit here and do nothing. "I'm going, with or without you."

12

"We are not going after him," Mackenzie said, still pulling on her snowsuit. I zipped up mine. "I mean it," Mackenzie insisted as I stomped into my boots. We were dressed in no time and leaving our room. "We are telling Ariadne what we've found." She punched the *up* arrow on the elevator.

I checked around the corner where I'd seen Blake disappear. "I want to know what he's up to and then we'll tell Grandma everything."

The *up* arrow dinged and the elevator doors opened. Mackenzie grasped my hand as if I was a toddler escaping from the playground and hauled me inside. She punched the button for Grandma's floor, still holding on to me.

I gritted my teeth. "We might be letting the killer get away."

"I might be saving your life," Mackenzie said. The doors opened, and I shuffled out, following Mackenzie. Floor-to-ceiling windows overlooked the courtyard. Blake was out there somewhere doing God knows what.

I almost laughed when I saw a figure in a red snowsuit appear outside right under the windows. "Grandma's not in her room," I told Mackenzie, who had already marched halfway down the hall.

"What, are you psychic now?" She cocked her head in that annoying way she did when she knew she was right, except this time she wasn't.

"Because she left the building." I punched open the stairway door. "Come on." I took the stairs two at a time. I had to wait for Mackenzie to catch up at the front door. We raced into the courtyard. Even in the thick snowfall, I spotted Grandma heading to the ice hotel. We followed.

"I don't like this." Mackenzie hurried forward. "What's Ariadne doing?"

It was still dark outside and snowy halos glowed around the lights. I'd always loved snow, the way it made the world seem so fresh and new. But after everything that had happened here, I felt as if the snow had created a barrier between us and the outside world.

The ice cathedral was ahead. At first I'd found it strange that the resort created a church of ice. Shauna told me couples paid big bucks to get married in what the Winter Wonder Resort called its ice cathedral – even though it was the same size as the little country church in my hometown. The first time I visited the cathedral I completely understood why it was such a big deal. The ice and snow gleamed in the twinkling lights that framed the interior. It was what I imagined heaven looked like. Sven had created a simple square ice altar with an amazing matching cross over it. But Sven's best work by far in the entire resort was a massive intricate icicle chandelier that hung in the centre of the cathedral. It was like a starry snowflake. You could look at it for ever and see some new detail every time. As I passed the ice cathedral, I was sure I saw the front door close. Is that where Blake had gone?

I stopped and suddenly felt the tug-of-war of common sense on one side and adventure on the other. I should follow Mackenzie who was following Grandma. The smart thing to do would be to tell Grandma and let her handle it. I took two steps towards the ice hotel, and then stopped again. The smart thing wasn't always my favourite option. I pivoted and headed towards the ice cathedral. Adventure always wins.

I slowly opened the front door to the cathedral an inch and peered inside. It looked empty. Maybe I'd only imagined the door closing. The snow and ice blended into a blanket of white and made it difficult to see sometimes. I yanked open the door and realized I was too late.

Blake was sprawled in the centre aisle. I rushed to him. That's when I saw smudges of red nearby. Blood. The blood-stained object took shape: it was a huge icicle. I followed the trail of blood to his head. His hair was matted with it.

"Blake, are you OK?" I bent down next to him. "Who did this to you?"

His eyelids fluttered open.

"Blake, it's Chase. What happened?"

His eyebrows crunched together as if he couldn't understand what I was saying.

He mumbled something. I leaned in so my ear was close to his lips.

"Revenge," he whispered. His hot breath tickled my ear.

"Revenge? What do you mean?" Did he mean he wanted revenge or did someone attack him to take revenge?

His eyelids drooped and then closed. Heat drained from my body. Was he dead? I removed one of my gloves and checked his neck for a pulse. His body was warm and I felt the thump of his heartbeat against my fingers. He was still alive. Relief flashed through me but only for a second.

I heard rustling at the back of the cathedral. I had been so intent on helping Blake that I didn't consider that the killer might still be here. There was someone, wearing the same snow gear as I was, standing with his back to me. I didn't think. I staggered towards the killer. Why was my instinct to always run head first into danger?

"Hey!" I shouted. Goggles covered half the killer's face and a black scarf covered the other half. I stopped a few feet away as I realized what the killer was doing. I followed the line of the rope in his hand up to the ceiling. He was untying the rope that secured the massive ice chandelier that hung right over Blake's unconscious body. What I thought was a heavenly snowflake transformed into a deadly weapon with spiky shards that would slice and dice Blake into a million pieces if it fell.

I was halfway between the killer and his victim. I spun around and dived for the baseball-bat-shaped icicle that had been used to knock Blake unconscious, just as the killer released the rope. It whizzed through the pulley, screeching as it went.

I snatched the icicle and swung it wide as the chandelier plummeted towards Blake. My icy bat connected with the chandelier, knocking it clear of Blake and shattering both into a million pieces. I used my body to shield Blake from the deadly shards that rained down.

When the ice storm stopped, the cathedral was empty. I considered racing after the killer, but I couldn't leave Blake alone.

"Help!" I screamed. "Someone help me!"

As I brushed the ice from Blake, I spotted a note clutched in his hand. I prised it out of his fingers. *Meet me at 7 a.m. in the cathedral.* So the killer lured Blake here.

I grabbed one of the spiky icicles that had once been part of the chandelier and stood over Blake. I was ready if the killer returned. I continued to yell for help.

Revenge. The word made me think of my mother. It had landed my mom in prison.

The door burst open. I shrieked like those stupid girls in horror movies. It was high-pitched and started at my toes, shuddered through my body and filled every millimetre of the ice cathedral. I cocked my arm ready to swing at the killer with all my might.

"Chase, it's me. It's Grandma." She charged down the aisle. The fear from moments ago drained away. The killer was gone. I was safe and so was Blake.

Grandma wasn't alone. Mackenzie, Sven, Shauna, Mr Ashworth and the security guards, the ones who were supposed to be guarding Lucinda's body, had barrelled in behind Grandma.

"Are you OK?" Grandma held me at arm's length and searched me from head to toe.

"I'm fine." I stepped aside so everyone could see Blake's body. "But he's not."

Grandma knelt down by Blake and gently inspected his injuries. "He needs medical help immediately."

Mr Ashworth spoke Swedish to the guards and they dashed off. "The resort has one vehicle that might be able to make it to the hospital. They are going to get it now. I've also asked them to alert Blake's grandfather."

Everyone gathered around, and I explained what happened. Mackenzie glared at me the entire time. When I finished, one security guard returned with Blake's grandfather. The other returned a few minutes later with this huge vehicle that was half SUV and half tractor. It had treads like a tank.

Mr Johnson held his grandson's hand as the guards carried Blake out and loaded him into the monster truck. Grandma made Mr Johnson promise to update us on Blake's condition.

"I need one of you to take Blake to the hospital and the other to stay here," Mr Ashworth explained to them.

"Both of us will go," one security guard said. "We didn't sign up for dead bodies." They hopped into the cab of the vehicle.

"No! No! One of you must stay here!" Mr Ashworth pounded on the side of the vehicle. Its engine roared. Mr Ashworth stepped back as it lurched forward. "At least let's hope they can make it to the hospital." He turned to Grandma and Shauna. "I'll call and update the police and see if we can't get an officer here soon. I'll ask my staff to deliver breakfast to each of the guests. We have no choice but to tell the guests to stay in their rooms until further notice. I'll draft a statement to distribute to everyone. We'll tell them it's for their own safety and due to the hazardous weather conditions. I'll organize the staff into teams and lead patrols of the resort."

"Thanks, Mr Ashworth," Grandma said.

Mackenzie punched me hard in the arm.

"Ouch!" I flinched away from her. "What was that for?"

"You left me." She punched me again, and I let her. It was a rotten thing to have done.

I rubbed my arm. "Sorry."

She punched me a few more times, but her blows had lost their power. "You could have been killed."

I didn't know what to say to that. She was right.

I trembled with the knowledge of what might have happened.

"From now on, we stick together," she said. "No matter what. Do you understand?"

I nodded. She was sort of scary when she wanted to be.

"I want you girls go to your room," Grandma said in her most bossy voice. "Maybe you could use this time to catch up with your schoolwork."

My dad had promised my school that I'd keep up with my studies online. Who could think of geometry or history at a time like this?

"But. . ." I started.

She continued to talk right over me. "Go to your room and lock the door." She glared at us. "I mean it. I don't want you poking around, looking in dumpsters or talking to anyone. This is serious."

Duh. She didn't know me at all if she thought I could be so easily sidelined. We could help. I knew we could. If it wasn't for me, Blake would be dead. I decided not to mention that fact.

"Sven, please escort Chase and Mackenzie to their room," Grandma said. "Girls, do not leave your room under any circumstances."

I knew there was no use arguing with her. We followed Sven to the lodge. Grandma didn't mean for us to hear it, but her voice swirled through the snowflakes. "What are we going to do, Shauna? Why is this happening? We are stranded here with a killer."

Revenge. I knew why it was happening, but what I didn't want to think about was . . . what would happen next.

13

“We’ve done it your way,” Mackenzie said as she switched on her computer and sat down at the desk. “Now we do it mine.”

“What’s your way?” I quipped. “We send our suspects strongly worded emails?” I flopped on the bed.

“We’ve been going about this randomly,” she said, without taking her eyes off her computer screen. “We need to think things through logically.”

I thought there was a dig at me in there somewhere. “OK. So what do you suggest?”

"We make a grid—"

I interrupted, "Oooo, a grid."

She glared at me. "Do you want to find out who is behind this or do you want to crack jokes?"

I shrugged. "I think I can multi-task, as you might say." I stood behind her.

"Motive, means and opportunity," Mackenzie said as she typed the titles into each column of the grid on her computer. "We create our suspect list and then assess if they could have done it and why."

"We know it has something to do with Ingenium International College," I said. Every terrible thing that had happened was swirling inside me. My body was vibrating with it. I started to pace. "Lucinda, Alexia, Mr Ashworth, Blake, TnT and loads of the guests have connections to that school."

"You're doing it again."

"What?" I shouted. "I'm being logical."

"You are jumping in at the middle," she explained. "Let's go through our suspects one by one."

I groaned. This was going to take for ever. We were stuck in here while the killer was escaping, or worse yet planning another murder. "Shall I list them alphabetically by height or favourite colour?"

"Stop taking the mickey."

"What?" Sometimes we really did speak different languages.

"Stop making fun of me. If you give my way a chance, we could solve the murder without disobeying Ariadne."

She was right and that burned even more. "Where do we start?"

"Everyone's a suspect until we rule them out."

"That's going to be a pretty long list." It felt pretty hopeless, but I kept moving and thinking.

Mackenzie stared at her computer screen, her hands poised over the keys. "We can't possibly know everyone's motives, but we can look at means and opportunity."

My face scrunched in confusion.

"Who had the ability and the opportunity to commit the crimes?"

Three short and sharp knocks on the door made us jump. "Are you girls OK in there?" Sven called through the door. Grandma must have asked him to check on us.

"Yeah, we're fine," I called. "What about Sven?" I whispered to her.

She typed his name at the top of the chart. "Means?"

"He's young. He's strong. He owns those scary looking carving tools. He knows this place because he helped build it."

She typed everything I said in the grid. "Opportunity?" she asked.

"He constructed the ice bed where Lucinda was found?" I said.

"And he was one of the first to arrive at the ice cathedral when you were screaming for help."

"What about poisoning Alexia?" I asked. "Did you see him at the party?"

"No, but he could have sprinkled on the fish flakes earlier. And just because we didn't see him doesn't mean he wasn't there. The problem with this place is that we all look the same in our Winter Wonder snow gear."

"He doesn't have any connection to Ingenium International College," I added and walked behind her so I could see what she was doing.

"That we know of." She typed furiously.

We both gasped when a mugshot of Sven appeared on the computer screen. We must have been louder than I thought, because Sven knocked on the door again. "What is going on?" he called and jiggled the door handle.

Did he have a master key? "We're changing clothes!" I called and pressed my body against the door as if that might stop him. We didn't need him barging in and seeing his name at the top of our suspect list.

"OK. Sorry."

I looked through the peep hole. He sat down across from our door and closed his eyes. He was standing guard. Had Grandma asked him too? He didn't seem too bothered that a killer was on the loose. Maybe because he was the killer. I tiptoed to Mackenzie.

"Sven Thomsen," she whispered, "was convicted

of breaking and entering when he was a kid. He was sentenced to a rehabilitation program, which seemed to turn his life around. In the last few years, he's won loads of awards for his ice sculptures."

"How can you possibly know all that? His mugshot and criminal history can't be on the internet."

She smirked. "You can find almost anything if you know where and how to look."

Sven wasn't the only criminal around. I was pretty sure that Mackenzie was breaking a few laws. Having a hacker as my best friend was proving to be very helpful.

"Any connection to Ingenium?" I asked.

"Not that I can find."

"Any connection to Alexia, Lucinda or Blake?"

"Nothing."

"So he's an ex-con, but not a killer."

"We can't rule him out. He has plenty of means and opportunity."

"But no motive."

"That's the tough part. He's got no motive that we

can find, but it doesn't mean he doesn't have one."

"Who's our next suspect?"

"Katrina has a motive even if we don't know what it is." Mackenzie typed Katrina Memering under Sven's name. "We saw her fighting with Alexia and later cuddling Blake. Who are you, Katrina Memering?" Mackenzie's fingers flew over the keyboard. She clicked on links, opened databases, processing the info and moving on before I could understand what she'd done. If there was a world championship of hacking, I bet she'd win the top prize.

"Very strange," Mackenzie muttered.

"What?" I said. Mackenzie didn't seem to hear me. "What?!" I said it louder this time.

"All I can find is information on her current job, articles she's written for a variety of magazines and clients. I can't find any connection to Ingenium International College or anything more than a few years old."

This reminded me of my struggle to find out more about my mom. "What if she's like Ariadne?

Ariadne uses her maiden name. What if Memering is her married name or her mom's maiden name or a name she made up?"

I paced the room again. Mackenzie clicked and tapped madly for a few minutes. "You are a genius!"

I smiled. No one had ever called me that before.

"I searched variations on the name Katrina and then checked birth certificates based on the bio on her website then I cross-referenced social media with—"

I stopped in front of her. "Yeah, yeah, but what did you find?"

"Katrina Memering used to go by the name of Trina Blanchett, and I need a drum roll please. . ."

"Get on with it!"

"Trina Blanchett went to Ingenium at the same time as Alexia and Blake."

"*You* are a genius!" I said as we high fived.

"Means and opportunity?" Mackenzie asked.

My excitement fizzled. "She couldn't have sabotaged the dogsled. She arrived after that happened."

Mackenzie thought for a moment. "She said her plane was delayed, but we only have her word for it. She could have arrived a day or two earlier."

"Or she could have hired someone to do it too," I added. As hard as it was for me to believe, people did that.

"What about when Alexia was poisoned?" Mackenzie asked when she'd finished typing our notes in her grid.

I remembered the moments before Alexia was poisoned. "The plate of food that Alexia ate from was originally Katrina's. Don't you remember they argued right before Alexia collapsed?"

"Actually Katrina handed her plate to Shauna and Alexia snatched the plate from her."

"Yeah, yeah, but the point is she had time to sprinkle the fish flakes on the plate. In the commotion she had plenty of time to throw away the vial of fish food."

"So you are saying she poisoned her own food in the hopes that Alexia would pick a fight and take her plate?"

"When you say it like that it doesn't make any sense."

"Do you think Katrina is allergic to shellfish too? It's a common allergy."

"Or maybe there was poison in the vial. We haven't analysed the contents. Maybe someone used the smelly fish flakes to cover up the poison."

"But Alexia recovered when you gave her that shot."

"We don't know what's happened to her since she left the resort, do we?" My brain was putting the clues together. "Maybe Katrina was the real target."

"Or the killer," Mackenzie added.

"We know one thing for sure," I said. "Katrina is mixed up in this." I handed Mackenzie her snowsuit and started to slip into mine.

She hugged her snowsuit. "What are you doing? Ariadne said we are not to leave this room. What are you thinking?"

I tugged on my boots. "That Sven is guarding our door so we'll have to leave by the window." I yanked it open and the icy air stung my cheeks.

Luckily we were on the ground floor.

"We agreed that we would stick together." She threw her snowsuit at me.

"I know." I threw it back. "So come on."

"Sticking together means that you stay here with me." Mackenzie crossed her arms across her chest as if tying herself in an immovable knot.

"Sticking together means you don't let me go out there on my own," I said, and climbed out of the window. I paced in the deep snow making two trenches as I waited for Mackenzie. I made it all the way to the end of the building. I peered around the corner. Two snow-suited figures were heading this way. I ducked back out of sight. I'd been spotted. If that was Grandma or Shauna I would be in the biggest trouble of my life. They'd probably lock me in a broom closet somewhere until this was over. I dashed to our window as Mackenzie was climbing out.

"We knew you two would be up to something."

I recognized the voice – TnT.

"What are you doing here?" Mackenzie asked.

Then I had a sickening thought. Mackenzie was right. We should have finished our list. It would have definitely included TnT. They were always sneaking around and running off. They attended Ingenium.

"What are *you* doing?" Toby, or was it Taylor, asked right back. "We heard about what happened to that Blake guy. Whatever you are up to, we're in!"

I didn't know if we could trust them. They were our age. Could they really be murderers? I knew age didn't matter. Teenagers killed all the time. Were they smart enough to have planned one murder and two attempts? I studied them. They'd played those pranks on us. That took planning – and there were two of them. Together I was sure they were capable of a lot.

"We were going to follow Sven," I lied. Mackenzie narrowed her eyes in confusion but didn't say anything. "He's got a criminal record, did you know that?"

"No," the boys said in unison.

"He's guarding our door, but we thought maybe we should watch him."

"Sort of like a stake-out," one boy said. They bounced with excitement.

"Yeah," I said. "Can you keep an eye on him and report back?"

They nodded. "What are you going to do?"

"You guys are much better at this kind of stuff," I said but one hundred per cent did not believe it. "We'll stay in our room. We aren't supposed to leave anyway."

As the boys dashed off, Mackenzie started to climb in the window.

"What are you doing?" I asked.

"I thought you said—"

"I'm not sure we can trust them. I needed them out of the way."

"So we are still going to disobey Ariadne and hunt for the killer," she said with a groan. She thought that by saying it matter-of-factly like that I'd see the crazy of my ways.

Nope.

I said, "Yep!" without hesitation. Because what she forgot about me was that I liked crazy.

14

We tried Katrina's room. She wasn't there or didn't answer. We searched the lodge floor-by-floor, careful to avoid anyone else who was skulking about. We checked every conference room, stairwell and maintenance closet. We even did a sweep of the perimeter of the lodge. No trace of Katrina. We ended up outside the front doors of the lodge.

"Can we please go to our room now?" Mackenzie whined.

"Maybe she's hiding at the ice hotel or the maze?" I suggested.

"No way. Not a chance. Don't even think about it." Mackenzie backed away from me, shaking her head. "Lucinda's body is still there frozen like a human ice cube. Last time I went there, you left me and nearly got killed." She stomped her boots in the snow as if she was planting herself.

"OK," I mumbled. I hated to give up and this felt like coming in last place in a tricycle race. I opened the front door a crack. The lobby was empty except for Shauna, who stood in the middle of the room surrounded by boxes. She was muttering to herself as she packed away Love Late in Life folders, travel mugs, key rings and brochures. No one was at the reception desk. I gestured my plan to Mackenzie using two walking fingers to represent us. *Crawl to desk. Hide under.* I mimed. Mackenzie shook her head, but followed me anyway.

"I can see you," Shauna said when we were only a few feet from the reception desk. We stayed crouched down as if she might forget we were there. "Come out for goodness' sake," she said with a sigh.

We walked over. After hours of snooping, it felt strange to walk normally again. "Don't tell Grandma," I said.

"What are you girls doing out of your room?" she asked.

I picked up a travel mug and traced the Love Late in Life logo. Shauna had worked so hard to make sure everything was perfect. We'd had endless memos and meetings about how everything would run once the guests arrived. She had left nothing to chance. But she didn't account for some crazy person running around hurting people. I imagined the killer's agenda: *Midnight: turn former headmistress into an ice cube. Noon: poison annoying mean girl with fish food. 7 a.m.: crush Blake under an ice chandelier.* I could have never guessed what would happen when we were stuffing these press kits and filling the travel mugs with snowflake- and heart-shaped chocolate.

"We thought you might need some help?" I said, counting on my truth-adjusting skills.

"Really?" Shauna said, raising one eyebrow.

Mackenzie looked from me to Shauna. "We can't find Katrina." She wasn't a bender of truths.

"Why on earth are you looking for Katrina?" she asked, her voice squeaking a bit higher.

I didn't know how to answer that question. *She's the main suspect in our murder investigation*, wasn't really the right answer.

"She, uh, I promised her . . . um. . ." Mackenzie started.

That was all I needed to form our excuse. "Mackenzie promised she'd give Katrina a behind-the-scenes look at Grandma's app for her story."

"I doubt there will be any article about the app now," Shauna said. "I've already started working on another strategy to rename and relaunch the app after all this is over."

I hadn't really realized until then that all this was probably killing Grandma's business and maybe Shauna's career too. "Let us try to help," I begged. "Do you have Katrina's phone number? We could make sure she's not filing any story that could hurt the app."

"You need to leave this to the grown-ups," Shauna's event-planner perkiness was long gone.

My insides burned at her comment. Grown-ups weren't the only ones who could do things. My quick thinking had saved Alexia's and Blake's lives. If I'd left it to the grown-ups, two more people would be dead.

"I'm worried about her," I tried again. "Can you at least check in on her?"

Shauna dug around in her messenger bag and found her phone. She hit the home button, which illuminated a picture of two girls about my age on the screen. She hit the button again but nothing happened. "This horrible thing is frozen again." She tossed the phone in her bag.

"Can I take a look?" Mackenzie said, holding out her hand. "Maybe I can fix it."

I suppressed a groan. What was Mackenzie doing? This wasn't going to help our investigation. I glanced at my watch. We really shouldn't hang out here any longer. Grandma could show up any minute, and we were standing here *wilfully disobeying* as my dad would say. It was one thing to be caught sneaking around. If she caught us standing here chatting away to Shauna, then it looked like we didn't care about Grandma's rules. I cared – I just didn't want to follow them.

"My phone is probably ruined like everything else," she said but fished out the phone and handed it to Mackenzie anyway. Mackenzie rebooted the phone.

"That's a nice picture," I said when Shauna's phone lit up again.

Something changed in Shauna's expression. She swallowed hard. "That's my best friend when I was in school."

Before I could ask anything else, Mackenzie swiped the photo away to reveal the keypad. "Can you enter your pass code?" she asked. Shauna tapped in her code. Mackenzie worked her magic, swiping screens and clicking and tapping. "All fixed."

"Thanks," Shauna said, punching a few buttons to be sure. I thought she might reward us and call Katrina, but no. She ditched the phone in her bag.

"I'll call Katrina as soon as I've finished packing everything," she said. "You girls shouldn't worry."

I wasn't going to give up that easily. As I turned to go, I intentionally knocked Shauna's messenger bag off the box where she'd placed it. The contents of both bag and box went flying across the floor. I might as well use my clumsiness as an asset. "I'm so sorry," I said, diving to the floor. I spotted her phone first and crawled towards it. "We'll pick up everything." I palmed the phone and shoved it into my pocket.

Mackenzie, Shauna and I scrambled on the floor, shuffling the Love Late in Life stuff into the box and everything else into Shauna's bag. "We better go." I hooked my arm through Mackenzie's as we left the lobby. Good thing Shauna wasn't paying much attention. She never questioned why we went back out the front instead of through the lobby. She didn't know a criminal was guarding our room and

TnT – two potential criminals – were watching him.

"I feel sorry for Shauna," Mackenzie said once we were outside our window again.

"Yeah, me too," I said and removed Shauna's phone from my pocket.

"You didn't," Mackenzie said when she saw the phone.

"We can call Katrina ourselves," I said. "We'll return the phone when we're finished."

"And say what?" Mackenzie was really annoyed with me.

"I'll think of something," I told her and swiped the screen. "Argh!" I grunted as the screen changed to the keypad with a message to enter a pass code. How could I have been so stupid? I'd stolen her phone for nothing. I didn't think my plan through. The phone needed her pass code. If we tried to guess, it would lock.

"Just so you know, I don't approve." Mackenzie punched in four numbers. The keypad transitioned into the homepage of Shauna's phone.

"How did you do that?" I asked in awe of my computer genius friend. "Are you a code breaker?"

Mackenzie shrugged as if she cracked super top-secret codes all the time. "No, I watched Shauna when she typed in her code earlier and remembered the numbers."

I hugged her. "You don't want to admit it, but you are as sneaky as I am."

Mackenzie smiled this huge toothy smile. She didn't often cut loose like that and I liked it.

I clicked on Shauna's contacts, found Katrina and dialled. I held the phone between us so we could both listen.

Katrina answered the phone and immediately started yelling. I was surprised by her response. It took me a minute to understand what she was shouting. Something about enough was enough. It was over and she wanted to go home.

"Katrina," I interrupted her rant. "Katrina, this isn't Shauna. This is Chase, Ariadne's granddaughter. We met when you first arrived."

"Oh," Katrina said.

"We've been looking for you," I said. "Is everything OK?"

She made some sound that was between a laugh and a grunt. "How can you even ask that with everything that has happened?"

Argh! She was right. I was being stupid again. I looked to Mackenzie for help.

"Could we meet up?" Mackenzie said, taking the straight-forward approach.

"Why?" Katrina asked.

"We are checking in with all the guests," I said.

The line was silent.

I decided that maybe now was the time for truth. "We think you know something about why this is happening."

"Meet me in thirty minutes behind the ice maze," she said and hung up.

I couldn't believe it worked.

"You were right," Mackenzie said. "She knows something."

"Hey! Stop!" The shouting was coming from the courtyard.

What was going on? More shouting. From more than one person. I tucked Shauna's phone in my pocket. We raced to the courtyard in time to see Sven running for his life with TnT hot on his heels.

15

I cringed as TnT tackled Sven and tumbled in the snow. That had to hurt. Mackenzie and I raced over as fast as we could in our clunky boots and puffy snowsuits.

"What do you think you're doing?" I yelled when I reached the pile of boys on the ground.

"We caught the killer," one twin said.

"Killer?" Sven shouted and squirmed away from TnT. "I am no killer."

"Then why are you trying to escape?" the other twin asked.

"I want to get away from you," Sven said as he stood and dusted the snow from his suit.

The twins each grabbed one of Sven's arms and hung on for dear life. "Not going to happen," TnT said together as if rehearsed.

"Who are you?" Sven asked.

"I'm Toby."

I studied him. They were the two most identical, identical twins I'd ever seen, but I couldn't keep thinking of them as TnT.

"I'm Taylor."

My focus shifted between the boys until I solved this real-life spot the difference puzzle. Taylor was a tiny bit bigger than Toby. Also there was something about their noses that wasn't identical. I made a mental note of who was who.

"I went to the toilet in the bath house," Sven explained. "I noticed someone following me. I tried to get away but these two chased me so I ran."

"Did you murder Lucinda?" Toby demanded.

"Did you bash Blake?" Taylor accused.

"No." Sven tried to twist out of the twins' grasp, but it was no use.

Toby and Taylor were botching my interrogation. I wanted to handle this just right. They were like a gaggle of toddlers in a cotton candy factory. "We know about your past," I said. I wanted to be vague. I meant his criminal history, but maybe there was other bad stuff about him I didn't know. I'd seen this tactic in a crime show once.

"So?" Sven replied.

"Makes you the prime suspect, don't you think?" I continued.

"You might as well give up," Toby said.

"Why did you do it?" Taylor asked.

I waved away their questions and stared at Sven.

"I knew that is what everyone would think," he said. "I lied to my employer about my past. It was long ago. I have changed. You must believe me."

"You were acting weird at your ice sculpture demonstration," I recalled. "And that was right before we found the body." I was convincing myself and the twins too of Sven's guilt.

"I found the frozen body of Lucinda," he said after a long pause. "I was scared. I didn't finish the ice bed so I sneaked back to finish the room. That is when I found her. I need this job. It could change everything for me. If Mr Ashworth fires me, what chance do I have with the other resorts?"

It made sense. I knew something about lying, and my gut told me he was telling the truth.

"What do you know about Ingenium International College?" Mackenzie asked.

"Why are you asking about that?" Toby said.

"In Jenny, um, what?" Sven shook his head. "I don't know anything. I never went to college."

Mackenzie and I exchanged the same look: *now what?*

"Should we lock him up?" Taylor asked.

Sven struggled in their grip.

"Lock him up?" Toby said. "We don't have an ice prison."

"Let me go!" Sven shouted and twisted free from the boys. "You cannot keep me here."

"No one is supposed to leave until the police arrive," Mackenzie said.

"I cannot wait for police. I cannot be accused." He tore off in the direction of the lake.

"Do we go after him?" Taylor asked.

I shook my head. "We can't keep him here."

"I believe him," Mackenzie said. "What motive could he possibly have for killing Lucinda and hurting Alexia and Blake?"

"A lot of killers don't have motives," Toby interjected.

"Yeah, look at all those serial killers," Taylor added.

I stopped them right there. I didn't need any more horrible thoughts in my already overactive brain. "I agree with Berkeley. He would be the prime suspect with his criminal history. Why would he put Lucinda in the bed he constructed? That would be stupid."

"Prisons are filled with stupid criminals," Taylor said.

Toby agreed. "I heard that there was this guy a few years ago that took a chainsaw—"

"Enough," I said. The word chainsaw started a slideshow of gruesome images in my brain. I didn't want to hear another word.

We heard the sound of an engine and then saw Sven blasting away on one of the snowmobiles. Maybe we should have gone after him, but if he was the killer, I was happy he was leaving and if he was innocent then I didn't mind that he was getting away either.

"That's one suspect down," Toby said.

"Now what?" Taylor asked. The boys bounced up and down. "This is the most excitement we've had since we were expelled."

Expelled? That was news to me.

Toby punched Taylor in the arm. "Idiot," he muttered.

I gulped. "Didn't you say you went to Ingenium?"

"Yeah," Taylor said and received another punch from his brother.

"Can't you keep your mouth shut?" Toby said to Taylor.

I suddenly realized the only thing we knew

about these two was that they went to Ingenium, and one of the only things I believed about this whole bizarre mess was that it was connected to Ingenium somehow.

"What are you two really doing here?" I asked.

Mackenzie stepped next to me. "We know you're hiding something."

We do?

"We got kicked out of Ingenium," Taylor said and received his third punch. "Hey, cut that out. It doesn't matter if they know."

"Why?" I asked.

Now Toby spoke. "We played a few too many pranks and our grades weren't that great anyway."

"Pranks like a dead body." I realized my mistake. I'd let slip what I really thought – they were suspects. I tried to recover. "I mean, a fake finger in the ice."

TnT clutched each other and nearly fell to the ground with their convulsive laughter.

"What's so funny?" Mackenzie asked.

"You guys think we're suspects," Toby said between laughing fits.

"You are always sneaking around and getting into trouble," I added, a bit annoyed that they were laughing at us.

"We are infamous criminals." Taylor burst out laughing again.

"I guess it's better than dropouts," I said. That shut them up.

"It's a little strange for you guys to be here with no parents or guardians or supervision," Mackenzie said.

"We couldn't hurt anyone," Toby pleaded.

"Seriously? Us, the killers?" Taylor added.

Mackenzie checked her watch and nudged me. "We need to go," she whispered.

"Where are you going?" Toby asked.

"None of your business," I said.

"You might as well tell us or we'll follow you," Taylor said.

They could spook Katrina and ruin everything.

Maybe it would be better if we knew where TnT was at all times. I sort of trusted them, but there was more to their story. Were they seeking revenge on people from Ingenium as payback because the school kicked them out? That seemed a little extreme, but as they pointed out, criminals could be stupid. I waved them into a huddle. "Mackenzie and I are meeting someone who may have information about the bad stuff that's been happening."

"Cool," Toby said.

"We're in," Taylor added.

Mackenzie was glaring at me in her *you're crazy* way.

"We need you two to stand guard," I explained. "This person can't see you or it could ruin everything."

"Got it," Taylor said.

"We are meeting behind the ice maze," I told them. "You go through the maze and wait at the back wall."

"Do we need a signal?" Toby asked.

"How about if we scream for help?" Mackenzie said and rolled her eyes.

"Perfect," Taylor said. Mackenzie's sarcasm was wasted on him.

*

"I'm getting out of here," was the first thing Katrina said when she showed up at the maze as arranged. She checked behind her every few seconds. "I'm leaving here one way or another and you better not do anything to stop me."

"OK," I said. This was starting to seem like a very bad idea. She was already threatening us.

"We know you went to Ingenium International College," Mackenzie blurted. Why did Mackenzie pick now to become the interrogator? "We know you went there with Alexia. We heard you fighting with her not long before her accident."

Katrina's expression shifted from anger to fright. She was hiding something.

"You would be smart to stop asking questions about Ingenium." Katrina poked me in the chest. I stood my ground. I wasn't about to let her see how scared I was. "Some things are better left in the past."

"Like what?" Mackenzie asked.

"It's all going to come out eventually," I said as if I knew more than I did. "Lucinda, Alexia, Blake and you are connected to Ingenium. When the police arrive, they are going to figure it out."

"I'm going to be long gone before the police show up," she said. "I'm not going to be next."

"Next?" I echoed. Was she being clever? Did she want us to believe she might be the next victim? She wasn't acting like a victim.

"You lured me here," she said, but the way she said it made me think she wasn't talking about our meeting. "You're probably mixed up in it." She backed away. "Just leave me alone. I didn't do it. I didn't do any of it."

"Then stay and help us find who did," I said.

"Help us," Mackenzie repeated.

Two screaming figures leaped down from the wall of the ice maze. We shrieked and kicked and punched and. . .

"Stop it!" the boys yelled.

While Mackenzie and I had lunged at the attacking figures, Katrina had taken the chance to run away.

"Why did you do that?" I shouted at them.

"You said *help*," Toby explained.

"But we didn't mean help," Mackenzie said.

"How were we supposed to know?" Taylor asked.

"She's getting away," I pointed out. "She's the key to figuring this out."

"She might be the killer," Mackenzie said.

"Leave it to us," Toby said.

"We'll catch her," Taylor added.

TnT bolted after Katrina. She was headed towards the forest, leaving snowy tracks as she ran. She was fast, but the boys were faster. I hoped we hadn't put the boys or Katrina in danger.

16

"What in the hell do you think you are doing?" Grandma's voice shot through the cold like an ice dagger. She stormed through the courtyard from the ice hotel.

We'd almost made it to the lodge. We froze in our tracks.

"This is not a game," she shouted when she reached us. "People are dead. Do you understand that? Dead."

Mackenzie and I bowed our heads and listened to the rest of her lecture. We were reckless and had disrespected her. Her face was glowing with anger. "And what if. . ." Her voice trailed off.

There were a lot of pretty awful *what ifs*.

"Sorry," Mackenzie said.

"Yeah, sorry," I echoed.

She marched us through the lobby continuing her lecture. "You are just like your mother," she blurted.

Was that an insult or compliment? I felt this weird combination of annoyance and pride. "How?" I asked.

"Bea couldn't let anything go." It was as if Grandma's anger had flipped off the sensor that usually stopped her from talking about my mom. "Once she got the bit in her teeth there was no stopping her. She always thought she could fix things. If there was a wrong to be righted, Bea thought she could do it. Her problem was she didn't care about the law. She thought good people should have justice. Bad people should get what they deserve."

"Is that why she's in prison?" I asked. "Was she some sort of avenger?"

"Oh, no you don't, young lady." Grandma stopped right in front of the elevators. "You will not aggrandize what she did. She's not a hero." Then Grandma looked me in the eyes for the first time since she caught us. "It started. . ."

"We know about Elizabeth," I said. I could see that time had not eased her grief.

"That's how Bea dealt with the death of her sister." Grandma's voice wobbled with sadness.

The elevator dinged and the doors slid open, slamming shut any further discussion about my mom. Grandma stepped inside. "Come with me."

"Um, Gran, our room is on the ground floor," Mackenzie said, sort of apologizing for being right.

"I know that." Grandma waved us inside. "That's how you escaped last time. This time you are going to my room on the top floor." She punched the button for her floor.

Mackenzie and I groaned. There'd be no way out. Mackenzie was probably thinking that she'd be without her precious computer.

"What was so important that you had to disobey me and risk your lives?" Grandma asked as we exited the elevator.

Mackenzie told her everything we'd learned, well almost everything. She managed to omit the really stupid parts about meeting with a would-be killer. My thoughts kept pinging back to my mom.

Grandma listened, but she gritted her teeth in frustration. She let us in her room and stood in the doorway. "You girls are to wait here, and I mean it this time. If I catch you outside this room, I promise that I will send the pair of you to the most isolated boarding school I can find. I'll make sure there will be no technology or athletics."

"We promise," Mackenzie jumped in.

"Aren't you going to stay with us?" I asked.

"I'm going to put an end to this once and for all," she said.

"I don't want you to go." I had that feeling again, the one that warns me when something bad might happen. "It's not safe for you to be out there on your own."

"I'm not going to let anyone else get hurt." The way that Grandma said it made me believe that she knew more than she was telling. "Do not open this door for anyone except me. Do you understand?"

Mackenzie and I nodded.

I hugged her. "I'm sorry," I whispered and really meant it this time. "Please be careful."

"I'll see you in a bit," she said, and shut the door behind her. The door handle jiggled as she tested to make sure it was locked tight, which it was.

"Now what?" I flopped on the leather couch. Her room was three times the size of ours. She had a living room, a bedroom with a king-sized bed, a little kitchen area and a bathroom with a Jacuzzi tub.

"Oh, no you don't," Mackenzie said. "I am not being banished to another boarding school. We are not leaving this room – neither one of us."

"I wasn't—"

"I know you, Chase. Ariadne is right. You can't leave it alone. How many near-death experiences do you need before you realize that sometimes doing nothing is the best course of action?" Her rant was almost as bad as Grandma's. "I'm going to use the Jacuzzi and clean up." She stormed off before I could utter another syllable.

With Mackenzie out of the way, I finally had some time to investigate, but for the first time in twenty-four hours I wasn't thinking about bodies in ice or motives or suspects. I pulled out my phone and typed in my mom's name. After some Mackenzie-like investigating, I'd found my mom's prison. I read almost every word on the prison's website. I tried to imagine her locked up. Because I'd never met her, I had a hard time picturing her. Grandma said I looked like her so I imagined myself behind bars. I didn't like how that felt. Being trapped in this deluxe suite was bad enough.

Mackenzie would have been proud of me. I'd learned a few things about hacking from her. I was eventually able to find an email address for the prison. It wouldn't go directly to my mom but maybe my message would reach her.

I clicked open my email as the *low battery* message flashed on my phone. My charger was in my room, and there was no way I was risking peeking outside the door. *Message for Beatrice Archer,* I typed in the subject line. I watched the cursor flash. I had no idea what I wanted to say. What do you say to the mother you've never met who is in prison for multiple homicides? I'm pretty sure there's not a web page for that and there's a web page for almost everything.

I typed *Hi Mom* and then deleted it. Do I call her mom? The little battery symbol on my phone switched to red. My heart started thumping. If I was going to send a message, I needed to do it quickly before I lost power. I didn't know when I'd have another chance to do this without Mackenzie looking over my shoulder. I felt my courage slipping away. What would Dad or Grandma say if they knew I was trying to contact my mom?

I decided to make the message short and direct. She might not even get it, and I didn't want the warden or whoever would read this message first to know too much about me.

I would be grateful if you would give this message to Beatrice Archer.

Hi! I bet you weren't expecting to hear from me since I've never heard from you.

Was that too mean? I left it for now.

This is Charlotte, but everyone calls me Chase. I'm your daughter.

Maybe she knew other Charlottes.

I would like to hear from you. Please email me back if you want to hear from me.

I thought about a million other things I could write, but I decided that this was enough for now.

Sincerely,

Chase

I hit send before I could change my mind. My phone screen went black. "Nooooooooooo!" I shouted. Had the message sent? Maybe it was a good thing that my ridiculous message was lost. What was I thinking? What a stupid message! I hoped it hadn't sent but a second later I wished it had. There was nothing I could do about it now either way. I slipped the phone into my pocket.

I clicked on the TV and flicked through the channels. I found an American cop show that they'd dubbed in Swedish. It was weird to see the actors' lips moving out of sync with the words being spoken. Mackenzie and I had tried to learn a few Swedish words from watching dubbed American shows. But so far all we learned was 'have you seen my dog' and 'you look beautiful'. I couldn't concentrate. I flicked off the TV. I was imaging the sixteen gazillion ways my mom could respond to my message. That is, if she even received it.

The worst thing would be if she didn't respond. Nothing. That was worse. If she wrote back and said that I should leave her alone, OK. Well, not OK, but at least I'd know. If she wanted to email me and find out more about me, I could decide if I really wanted to talk to her. I needed to stop thinking about it and imagining what could happen next, from visiting her in prison to her taking a hit out on me. Yeah, it wasn't logical but that sometimes happened with my overactive imagination. Overactive didn't mean smart or helpful, it just meant lots and lots of thoughts crashed around in my brain.

I was so wrapped up in my thoughts that I almost didn't hear it.

Click.

I sat bolt upright. That was the sound of the door unlocking. I waited for Grandma to bound into the room, but instead the door slowly edged open. That wasn't Grandma. She wouldn't sneak into her own room, not with everything that had happened.

I searched for something to use to defend myself. The first thing I spotted was a big blue and purple vase. I snatched it off the coffee table and tiptoed behind the door. I raised the vase above my head and watched as the door slid open one millimetre at a time.

17

A hooded head peeked through the open door. The vase dropped from my hands, missing the intruder by centimetres. It shattered into a million pieces with a thunderous boom.

I screamed.

Mackenzie screamed from the bathroom.

And TnT shrieked as they tumbled into the room.

"What are you doing?" I yelled at the pair and slammed the door behind them.

"Chase! Chase!" Mackenzie shouted from the bathroom. "Are you OK? What's happening?"

"Yes," I called through the bathroom door. "I'm fine. Toby and Taylor have stopped by."

They were brushing glass from their snowsuits and picking it off each other like a couple of monkeys.

Mackenzie emerged from the bathroom in a steamy cloud. In her hurry to dress, her shirt was turned inside out and backwards with the tag sticking out.

"Why did you let them in?" Mackenzie planted her hands on her hips and launched into a lecture. "What are you thinking? Ariadne said not to open the door to anyone, and—"

"I didn't open the door," I interrupted. I wasn't to blame for this.

"We used a key," Taylor said.

"How do you have a key?" I swept Mackenzie behind me.

"We *found* the passkey at reception," Toby said. "You aren't the only two who can snoop and spy on people."

"What happened to Katrina?" Mackenzie asked.

I gestured to the tag on her shirt. She tucked her arms in and spun the shirt around. It was still inside out but for once, she didn't seem to care what she looked like.

"We lost her in the forest," Toby said.

"She's got to come back eventually," Taylor added. "There's nothing around here. She'll get hungry or cold or—"

"Or dead," Toby said with a laugh, but no one else thought it was the least bit funny.

Taylor gave his brother a punch. "Idiot."

"You guys should leave." Mackenzie shooed them away like flies on potato salad.

"Don't you want to hear our great idea?" Taylor said with a mischievous grin.

I glanced at Mackenzie with raised eyebrows, asking what she wanted to do.

"Argh." She groaned. "OK, but you can't stay long. If Ariadne catches us, Chase and I are de. . . in big trouble."

She'd thought better of saying *dead*. It was strange that in our present situation *dead* wasn't a joke.

"You got a mini bar?" Toby asked and walked right over to the mini fridge. "I'm starving."

"You're not staying," Mackenzie said and slipped between Toby and the fridge.

"Harsh," Toby muttered.

Mackenzie and I sat on the two big purple leather chairs while TnT flopped on the matching couch.

"We've got the passkey, and we thought you might want to help us check out Katrina's room."

My expression must have given me away because Mackenzie said, "Not a chance. We are not leaving this room."

"Two of us can be the lookouts and two can check the room." Toby twirled the passkey between his fingers.

"No, absolutely not." Mackenzie walked to the door and opened it. "That's called breaking and entering."

"They do it all the time on TV," Taylor said. "I mean, if the person has committed a crime or you think they might commit another, or if someone might be hurt or need help."

"We could be saving lives," Toby said.

Sounded reasonable to me, but I stayed silent.

"Come on," Taylor whined. "We could find proof that Katrina is the killer and then we'll be heroes."

I studied Mackenzie. Her frown softened. Maybe they were getting to her. "No. Go," she said but I could tell she was having second thoughts.

We jumped when someone pounded on the door. TnT dived behind the couch.

"Who is it?" Mackenzie called through the door.

"It's Shauna."

Mackenzie mouthed, *what should I do?*

"What do you want?" I called to Shauna as I stepped next to Mackenzie.

"Let me in!" She was agitated.

"Um, Ariadne told us not to let anyone in," Mackenzie said.

"I've got a message from your grandma," Shauna replied and jiggled the handle. "And lunch."

I opened the door. Shauna marched into the middle of the room and dumped two Winter

Wonder gift bags on the table. The bags tipped over, spilling out sandwiches, potato chips and cans of soda. Snow was melting off her boots. She unzipped her snowsuit a bit. "Ariadne has gone for help. She told me to tell you not to worry. I begged her not to go. But you know your grandma."

We both nodded. That sounded like my stubborn grandma. She couldn't sit around doing nothing. Like grandmother, like granddaughter. Maybe that was what she meant about putting an end to it once and for all.

"I've gone door to door, delivering meals and asking our guests to remain in their rooms." She pointed to me and then Mackenzie. "That includes you too." She turned towards the couch. "And you two." The boys popped up, grinning. "You boys need to return to your room, or I'll tell—"

"Yeah, all right," Toby interrupted.

Who would she tell? As far as we knew, the boys were here on their own.

"Have you two seen my phone?" Shauna asked and looked straight at me. Maybe it was my guilty conscience, but it seemed as if she knew what I'd done.

"Why yes," Mackenzie said, slipping into her posh speak. "We found it in the lobby. We forgot we had it." Mackenzie retrieved the phone from the snowsuits piled on the floor.

Shauna unlocked the phone and tapped the screen. I tried to see what she was doing, but she held the phone close to her chest. If she checked the call history, she'd see that we had dialled Katrina. Shauna was making me nervous.

"Boys, out!" Shauna held open the door. The boys didn't move. "Now!" Toby and Taylor each snatched a sandwich from the table. She followed them out. They were gesturing and mouthing something behind Shauna's back but I had no idea what they were trying to tell us. They stopped as soon as Shauna flipped to face them. "You girls stay put." She glared at us. "I wouldn't want anything to happen to the two of you."

"Fine," I grunted, annoyed that she was treating us like five year olds.

"You'll let us know as soon as Ariadne returns?" Mackenzie asked.

"Of course," Shauna said and slammed the door in our faces.

I flopped on the couch, completely and utterly frustrated.

Mackenzie stood there.

"What is it?" I sat up straight.

"I don't know," she muttered. "Nothing."

"Tell me what you're thinking."

I could almost see her computer brain whirring. She went to the bathroom and returned with her phone. "I called and sent texts to Ariadne. She hasn't responded." She hit redial and tried Grandma again. It immediately went to voicemail. "Ariadne, please call me. We're getting worried," Mackenzie pleaded into the phone and then hung up. "Her phone is switched off. Why would she do that?"

"Her battery might have died," I said, remembering the email to my mom and my dead phone. *Dead*. That word punched worry in my gut. "Or she might not have a signal. You know there are dead spots all around here." *Dead.* I gulped at my stupid use of the word again.

The door lock clicked. There wasn't time to react. TnT walked in and shut the door behind them.

"Get out," I said what I thought Mackenzie would want me to. Toby reached for the door handle.

"Wait," Mackenzie said. My eyes widened in surprise.

"We made sure what's-her-face didn't see us," Taylor said.

"Time for some snooping." Toby held up the passkey.

"Let's go," Mackenzie said, and I couldn't have been more proud.

We dressed in our snowsuits again. They were bulky and awkward to move in, but this way, we looked alike. Even if we were spotted, no one could tell who we were with our hoods up. We took turns keeping a lookout and darting down corridors, stairwells and eventually into Katrina's room. Taylor kept the door open a crack and stood guard. Toby and I searched Katrina's room while Mackenzie zeroed in on her computer.

"Look at this," Mackenzie whispered after only a few minutes. We gathered around her. "Her computer wasn't locked. I scanned her recent history and this is what she's been working on."

Mackenzie was scrolling down a Word document. Big deal. We knew Katrina was a journalist. "So?" I said.

"Did you read it?" she asked.

"You were scrolling it too fast," Toby said.

"Is it her article about Grandma's app?" I asked.

"No, that's the weird thing," Mackenzie said and scrolled to the headline at the top of the document: *The Secrets We Keep.* "It's about a fifteen-year-old girl named Parker Stephens who drowned. It's only a page or two but it's written like fiction, not a newspaper article."

A dead girl. What did she have to do with anything? But then Blake's voice echoed in my brain: *revenge.*

"What was that?" Mackenzie asked, making the rest of us jump.

"I didn't hear anything," Taylor said and looked out of the door to be sure.

Mackenzie rushed to the window and peeked out. I took her place at the computer and read Katrina's story.

"What now?" Toby asked.

"I thought I heard someone outside," Mackenzie said, and traced the jagged scar on her neck. "Katrina could return at any minute. We shouldn't be here. I was wrong to go along with this. What was I thinking?" Mackenzie babbled when she got nervous.

Mackenzie kept talking. I kept reading. The story started with a fifteen-year-old girl's dead body being dragged out of a lake. For some reason the girl was covered in red and gold paint. Katrina wrote in such detail about the paint swirling into orange under the body. The final words of the story were: *They called it an accident and maybe it was, but it didn't need to happen.*

"Those are Ingenium colours," Toby said, pointing to the screen.

"What?" The hairs on the back of my neck prickled. Another deadly connection to Ingenium. The only name in the story was Parker Stephens. It read like a story in a book, but it felt eerily true. It can't be a coincidence that Katrina was writing this story now.

"Can we go?" Mackenzie was waiting at the door.

I shut down the computer. "OK," I said. I didn't

know if it was Mackenzie's sudden jittery behaviour or the story, but I felt it too. It was like a clock was counting down in my brain to some unknown horror.

"Help us return the key," Toby said. That was fair.

Like before, we tag-teamed to the lobby. One pair served as lookout. When the coast was clear the other pair moved. I was partnered with Taylor. As we waited in the stairwell for one of the bellboys to pass, I asked him, "Do you know anything about a dead girl drowning in a lake at Ingenium?"

The bellboy disappeared into the lobby so we waved Mackenzie and Toby forward.

"There's this school legend," he said as we waited for the all-clear signal. "I didn't think it was real. You know one of the stories the upper classmen tell the newbies to keep them from sneaking to the lake."

Mackenzie and Toby were hiding behind a potted pine right where the corridor from the rooms intersected with the lobby. Mackenzie signalled us forward. We crawled behind the reception desk and signalled Toby. He continued on; he had the passkey and was going to return it to the manager's office.

"What's the legend?" I whispered but kept my eyes glued to Toby.

"A girl haunts the lake seeking revenge on Ingenium students," he whispered.

There was that word again. "Why revenge?"

"The story goes that she was killed during some initiation thing, and—" His story was cut short by someone yelling in the lobby.

"How dare you!"

"Oh no," Taylor said as he walked from our hiding place.

I reached for him. "What are you doing?" I whisper-shouted at him, but he disappeared into the lobby.

"I will kill you two boys!" Was that Mr Ashworth's voice?

He had a connection to Ingenium. He knew Lucinda and had invited a bunch of people from

Ingenium here for Grandma's event. Was Mr Ashworth our killer? I hunched down next to Mackenzie.

Mr Ashworth had Toby and Taylor by their collars and was dragging them through the lobby. I didn't think I'd ever seen anyone so angry. "You two have been nothing but trouble," he shouted. "Why did you steal the passkey? What were you doing?" He was so angry his words were jumbling together, and spit and sweat were pinging off him.

We had to help TnT. I gestured to Mackenzie that she head one way and I'd go the other. He couldn't overpower all four of us.

Mackenzie and I darted from hiding, as Mr Ashworth shouted, "Tobias Horatio and Taylor Ignatius Ashworth, I am so ashamed of you!" Mackenzie and I dived behind the reception desk. "Kicked out of school and now this!"

Ashworth? Toby and Taylor Ashworth? They were the manager's sons. The yelling continued. The boys were in huge trouble, but not in any real danger.

"They've been lying to us this whole time about who they are and why they're here," Mackenzie said.

"Let's get out of here," I said. They were caught, but we didn't have to be. I flicked the hood of Mackenzie's snowsuit over her head.

"Oh no," she said when she realized Mr Ashworth was blocking the way to Grandma's room.

"No choice," I said and dashed to the front door. I punched it open and held it until Mackenzie stumbled out. We raced into the snow. The world was sparkly and beautiful but didn't feel safe any more. I didn't know if I was running to or from something. All I wanted was to run away.

"What are you doing?" Mackenzie pulled us to a stop. The ice maze was just ahead. The lake and the forest were beyond. Was my grandma out there somewhere? "I don't want to be out here. We are going to lock ourselves in Ariadne's room until she comes for us." Mackenzie's voice cracked. She was terrified.

"OK," I said. We took a few steps towards the lodge.

"Did you hear that?" Mackenzie said. I shifted so we were back to back. She wasn't making it up this time. I'd heard it too. Footsteps.

I froze. I saw something emerging from the snowy scene ahead of me. The image took shape. It was a person, but he wasn't wearing the standard issue blue-and-black Winter Wonder Resort gear. The figure was in some sort of high-tech silvery suit that almost blended with the wintery surroundings.

I took Mackenzie's hand and ran away from the figure. "In here," I said, when the ice maze came into focus. She checked behind us. We couldn't see the figure but we could still hear him approaching. "We can lose him in here," I told Mackenzie and manoeuvred her ahead of me.

She'd figured out the way to the centre of the maze in no time on her very first try. We'd been through it so many times that I knew we turned left by the big snowman, right by the ice sculpture with the massive snowflakes, straight on until we hit a dead end at an ice polar bear. That was the tricky part. There was a tunnel hidden behind the bear that was a shortcut to the centre.

We had the same idea at the same time. We ducked behind the polar bear and hid in the tunnel. I hoped the person chasing us didn't know the ice maze very well. We didn't dare speak. We knew that sound bounced off the glassy surfaces. Our panting breath clouded our view, but we saw the silvery figure skid as he reached the polar bear and dashed away.

I crawled out and watched as the figure headed deeper into the maze. I waited and counted the footsteps until I was sure he was far enough away. "Come on," I whispered in my quietest voice to Mackenzie. We tiptoed back the way we came, making as little sound as possible.

The entrance to the maze was in sight. We'd made it. "Race you to Grandma's room," I whispered.

We bolted forward but slid to a stop and crashed to the ground as a figure in a Winter Wonder Resort snowsuit stepped into the maze's entrance and blocked our only way out. We screamed, shattering the snowy silence. Our terror echoed and seemed to fill the maze. The figure's face was obscured by goggles and a scarf, just like in the ice cathedral. It was the same figure who had tried to kill Blake, I was sure of it. The killer raised his hands to reveal he was holding a sharpened dagger of ice in each hand – one for each of us.

19

I didn't wait for the killer to attack. I lunged for his middle and knocked him to the ground. He may have been bigger, but I'd surprised him by striking first. I staggered to my feet, quicker than my attacker. My dad told me that when the options are fight or flight, run like hell. I wasn't going to wait for round two. I stumbled out of the ice maze. I expected Mackenzie to be right behind me.

The killer was disappearing into the maze, and I realized too late that Mackenzie and I had gone in opposite directions – me towards danger and her away.

"Help! Chase!" Mackenzie was shrieking as she raced further and further into the maze. I followed the sound of her voice. She was heading towards the centre. She wouldn't have time to use the tunnel. She couldn't risk getting stuck in the narrow passageway.

The faster I ran the more I slipped and slid. I was crashing into the ice wall and losing time. I could still hear Mackenzie shouting for me. "I'm coming," I called.

I was so focused on Mackenzie that I didn't realize I was being followed until the silver-suited figure was practically on top of me.

Two killers? Was there a team of killers on the loose? My mind flicked to TnT, but it couldn't be them, could it?

I used my only real weapon again – the element of surprise. I spun around and threw a punch, but I misjudged everything. I only managed to nick my attacker as he passed and slammed me into the wall. I kicked off the wall and dived for his feet, but he swiftly and easily sidestepped my hands. I face-planted on to the ground. The packed snow gave me an icy burn on my cheek. I was stunned but not stopped. Why didn't my attacker finish me off? It didn't make sense. All I knew was that now both of the bad guys were after Mackenzie. Were these assassins sent to kill her? I ran.

When I reached the polar bear, I made a split-second decision to go up, not down. I leaped into the bear's outstretched arms and scrambled to its shoulders. I wrapped my arms around its neck to steady myself. If I could stand on its shoulders, I could see into the centre of the maze. I hoped I could spot Mackenzie and pinpoint her two attackers. From that vantage point, I'd have a better chance of helping Mackenzie. But it wasn't going to be easy.

The bad thing about using ice as your ladder was that it melted. The more I clawed at it the more slippery it got. I took a deep breath. The only way I'd manage to stand was using balance, not speed. I [illegible]d to calm down. My heart was beating so rapidly

I wondered if part of my ice-melting-slippery problem was that I was generating the heat of a volcano.

I positioned one foot but moved the other too quickly and fell flat on my back on the ground. The impact knocked the wind out of me, but a few seconds later, I'd catapulted myself up again. This time I took it nice and slow. I found one foot hold and balanced. Once on top of the polar bear, I moved to the maze wall, which was at least somewhat flat, and then slowly rose to my feet.

What I saw nearly sent me crashing to the ground again, but I steadied my breath. I stretched my arms for balance. The figure in goggles and the Winter Wonder Resort snowsuit had Mackenzie cornered in the centre of the maze with an ice dagger ready to strike. The figure in the silver suit had nearly reached the centre too. It was two adults against one helpless Mackenzie. She didn't have a chance. If I threw myself at one attacker, the other one could easily overpower me. I had one move, and I had to make the most of it. I'd wait until both attackers had reached the centre, and I'd try to take them out with a Chase Armstrong dive-bomb. I wasn't sure I could get much leverage on the ice. I needed to hit them with force, not simply fall on top of them.

I hunched down, preparing to attack, but the strangest thing happened. The silver-suited figure burst into the opening and pounced on Mackenzie's attacker. The two baddies crashed to the ground. I saw my chance.

"Up here!" I shouted to Mackenzie. She was trembling so badly it was hard for her to walk. "Focus on me," I told her, but we kept glancing at the two mysterious figures who were engaged in an all-out brawl.

I straddled the wall and reached down for Mackenzie. She clasped my hand with both of hers. Together I hoisted and she climbed, and at last, she was sitting next to me. She tried to hug me but I batted her away. "Look!"

The goggled figure who had threatened ...kenzie with the ice dagger had broken free and was racing out of the maze. The man in the silver suit was hot on his heels.

"We can't let them get away," I told Mackenzie and pulled her to her feet.

"Are you crazy?" Mackenzie shouted. "Of course we can."

"We need to stop this once and for all." That's what Grandma had said the last time we saw her. We needed to find out who was after Mackenzie or they would just keep coming. I hopped down and raced after them. Soon I could hear the crunch of Mackenzie's steps behind me.

As we burst through the maze's exit, I spotted the two figures heading towards the lake. The moment Mackenzie caught up to me, I grabbed her hand, and we followed. She protested with every step, but TnT had lost Katrina once, and I wouldn't let her get away again.

Katrina.

Her name had popped into my brain like the answer to a multiple-choice test question. That's who I thought was behind those goggles. I had no idea who was following her in the silver snowsuit, but I was going to find out.

On the lake's shore was a line of snowmobiles. We were in the middle of nowhere and the resort kept the keys in the ignitions. I thought they were crazy, but Mr Ashworth said they'd never lost a snowmobile – until now.

The baddies wasted no time. They each stole a snowmobile and zipped off around the lake and into the snowy fog. They sort of resembled astronauts in their snowsuits and helmets.

"Hop on," I told Mackenzie when we reached a snowmobile. I chucked a helmet and goggles at her and strapped mine on.

"I'm driving." Mackenzie slipped to the front of the seat. I didn't have time to argue, although my stomach lurched at the memory of her horrible yacht-driving skills in the Maldives.

I jumped on behind her and hooked my arms around her middle as we took off with a jolt. "Follow those snowmobiles!" I shouted.

But she didn't.

"What are you doing?" I shrieked. Could she hear me? I leaned forward and pointed to the snowmobile tracks that veered around the lake's edge. She shook her head and steered us straight on to the lake.

"They're getting away," I screamed. I clutched her arms and tried to steer the snowmobile in the right direction, but she elbowed me away. I slid on the seat and wrapped my arms around her middle again to keep from being flung off.

If she wanted to go for help, why wasn't she heading to the lodge? All that was ahead of us was the lake and then miles of wilderness. Maybe her near-murdered experience had caused her to snap. I couldn't blame her if she'd lost her mind. I hadn't had the dagger to my throat and I was pretty freaked out by this whole ice-murder thing.

I hugged her waist in my attempt to tell her everything was OK. I understood. She was right not to follow the bad guys. What was I going to do if I caught them anyway? Once again, Mackenzie's logic had probably saved my life.

We bounced across the frozen lake. We hit a bump and skidded one way and then the other. Mackenzie gripped the handlebars of the snowmobile, and I held on to her for dear life. We nearly tipped over, but we managed to lean our weight in the opposite direction. We slammed back on to the ice. I was surprised when she didn't slow down. She actually revved the engine.

She pointed straight ahead.

"Woohoo!" I shouted as I realized that she had taken a shortcut across the lake, and we were on a collision course with the bad guys.

Dead ahead a snowdrift blocked our way. I would have known to veer around it. But Mackenzie bore down and tried to power through it. *Big Mistake!* The problem was what looked like a harmless pile of snow was actually a ramp of ice. We charged up it and. . .

"AAAAAAAAAAHHHHHHHHHHH!!!!!!!!" we screamed as we became airborne. I leaned us [illegible]ward and flattened us as much as possible to the [illegible] crashed down again.

"Woohoo!" Mackenzie shouted.

I would make a daredevil out of her yet.

But our victory was short-lived.

CRACK!

The sound like thunder came from below, not above, us. We scanned our surroundings searching for the source of the sound. Mackenzie turned her head and the handlebars simultaneously, zigzagging us along the lake.

I held her shoulders forward to send her the message to drive straight. She did. I glanced back and wished I hadn't.

I understood immediately what the cracking sound was. A huge hole had opened in the lake's surface where we had crash-landed.

But that wasn't the worst thing.

The worst thing was that our speeding snowmobile was acting like a zipper and splitting an icy crevice through the frozen lake.

"Faster!" I shouted to Mackenzie.

She shook her head.

I debated whether to tell her about our deadly

dilemma. Would she hear me through her helmet and over the roar of the engine? I wished I didn't know that we were only a few feet away from an ice-watery grave.

CRACK!

"Faster!" I shouted again. Mackenzie must have realized what was happening, because the snowmobile lurched forward and jerked me backwards with the force of our speed. My head slammed the seat behind me. I viewed the scene upside down, but the danger was unmistakable. We were barely outrunning the breaking ice!

20

My stomach churned and threatened to turn inside out as Mackenzie pushed the snowmobile to its max. I imagined the lake opening and swallowing us into its icy depths. We'd be weighed down by the snowmobile and our snow gear. If we hit the water, we wouldn't survive. Would we freeze or drown first? I didn't want to die that way. I didn't want to die PERIOD.

The snowmobile shuddered, making my teeth chatter. My body was slammed every which way, but I didn't care. The thick rough ice was the shoreline and it meant we were safe.

"Woohoo!" I shouted and loosened my death grip around Mackenzie. "You did it!" I dared a look behind me and nearly fell off. A huge hole had opened in the lake only a few feet from the shore. We must have been inches from being icicles.

With our focus on survival, we'd lost track of the bad guys. I scanned the forest ahead and glimpsed something moving too fast to be an animal. I pointed. Mackenzie nodded. Mackenzie revved the engine and took off. I guessed she didn't want us to have almost died for nothing. Between the shower of snow from the sky and the spray of snow from the chase, I could barely see. I wiped at my goggles and smeared water across my field of vision. I could only see one snowmobile. Maybe the other one was too far ahead or maybe it got away all together.

Mackenzie slowed to avoid crashing into trees. At this speed we'd never catch the bad guy. I think was the one in the silver suit. I spotted a clearing r right. Instead of following, we'd cut him pass. I pointed and shouted my idea to

Mackenzie who did exactly as I instructed.

Soon we were on a crash course with our attacker in silver. By the time the driver spotted us it would be too late. I positioned myself on the seat so I was ready to spring into action. The second Mackenzie steered in close enough, I charged at the silver-suited figure and knocked us both off. I expected a fight. I moved quickly, pinning the figure to the ground. I raised my fist, prepared to strike, but the figure raised his arms in surrender.

Mackenzie circled back and parked the snowmobile next to me and my prisoner. She tumbled off the snowmobile. She tossed her helmet and gloves and took huge gulps of air.

"Are you ready to meet the killer?" I asked Mackenzie. My hands were shaking with fear and excitement. Was this Katrina? I removed the helmet and goggles and gasped. It was a black woman I'd never seen before. Mackenzie stumbled over.

"Mum?" Mackenzie said and knocked me off the woman.

Wait . . . did she say *mum?*

In answer to my question, Mackenzie hauled the woman to her feet and collapsed into a hug. "Are you OK?" Mackenzie asked.

The woman nodded. "I've missed you so much." There was no question that they were mother and daughter. They had the same curly hair and facial features, except Mackenzie's mum was pumped up like an action figure while Mackenzie was Barbie.

This woman had something to do with sending my mom to prison. Mixed with the adrenaline from the chase was anger. I clenched my fists. Was the woman in front of me partially responsible for robbing me of my mom? The longer they hugged the more I felt the heat of my anger. *It wasn't fair.* That thought looped on repeat in my brain.

"What are you doing here?" I blurted. That got their attention. Their hug slipped into holding hands.

"Chase, this is my mum." Mackenzie bounced h excitement. "Mum, this is Chase."

ilyn," she said and extended her hand. I e and then rubbed my palm again and again on my snowsuit.

When I spoke, I tried to smooth the jagged edges in my voice. "Why were you chasing us?"

"You clever girl, you've spotted me a few times over the last few days, didn't you?" She smiled the same smile as Mackenzie.

So she was the stalker I'd seen lurking around the Winter Wonder Resort. I wasn't imagining things. "I told you someone was watching us," I said to Mackenzie.

"When I saw you leaving the lodge, I was finally going to talk to you," Mackenzie's mum continued. "But you ran away and then I saw that person chasing you..." She scanned her surroundings. "I shouldn't have come here, but after everything that happened in the Maldives, I had to see for myself that my beautiful girl was OK." She kissed Mackenzie on the cheek. "I know I'm supposed to be publically grieving for my *dead* daughter. I told everyone that I needed a break. You can't blame a mother for caring about her only child."

Ugh! They were hugging again. I'd never had any

experience with a mother-daughter relationship. I was happy for Mackenzie, but I also felt that all-too-familiar ping of jealousy I always felt with any mother-daughter thing. I remembered the email I'd sent to my mom.

Mackenzie rode with her mum and I followed on my own snowmobile. We went around the lake this time. We parked the snowmobiles where we'd found them.

"I must leave you two here," Marilyn said, but I could tell it was the last thing in the known and unexplored universe that she wanted to do. "I'm going to go for help. I'll watch until you are safely in the lodge. I want you to collect everyone in the lobby." She took Mackenzie's hand again. "If everyone stays together then you should be safe. Can you do that?"

I didn't nod. She couldn't show up and boss me around.

[illegible]Why don't you stay with us?" Mackenzie [illegible]

[illegible]a's missing," I told her. "Shauna said

Grandma was going for help, but we've tried calling her and she doesn't answer and she left a long time ago and there's a killer on the loose and. . ."

"I'll go for help and search for Ariadne," Marilyn said. "I'll drag the police here if I have to. I don't want you girls worrying about it. I'll take care of everything." She opened her arms, offering me a hug, but I flinched away.

"Thanks and whatever." I could take care of myself.

"You look so much like your mum," Marilyn said. "Looking at the two of you, it's like I'm looking at a picture of me and Bea when we were your age."

It hurt for her to talk about my mom. I vowed that Mackenzie and I wouldn't turn out like our moms. We would stay friends for ever.

They hugged again.

"Come on," I told Mackenzie.

"You need to go," Marilyn said. I pulled Mackenzie away.

"Be careful," she told her mum.

"Love you," they said at the same time.

Gross!

Mackenzie and I walked to the lodge in silence. At least we'd solved one mystery.

We could hear shouting before we even entered the lodge.

"Enough!"

Mackenzie and I flinched at the anger in the shouted voice. Was that the voice of a killer? The lodge's lobby was deserted. We crouched behind the reception desk and then crawled around it.

"I expect this entire storage area to be ship-shape by the time I return."

I recognized Mr Ashworth's voice. Mackenzie and I dived into the nearest office when we heard his pounding footsteps heading our way. We waited until he'd stomped across the lobby before w[illegible] approached the storage room.

[illegible]oks like we can cross the Ashworths off our [illegible]t," Mackenzie whispered to me when we [illegible] of the storage room. Everything had been pulled off the shelves. The boys were crawling around on the floor arranging the snow boots by size.

I nodded. "They must have been here since we left."

"Hi," I said as Mackenzie and I stepped into the room.

"What are you two losers doing here?" Toby said. "I thought you'd have caught the killer by now."

"We were almost the next victims," Mackenzie said.

Both boys were on their feet and at our side. "Really?" "Are you OK?" "What happened?" They fired questions at us, and we answered every one.

"Have you guys been trapped in here with your dad this entire time?" I asked, not so subtly double-checking their alibis.

They nodded.

Then I remembered the conversation that was cut short with Taylor. "You were telling me about the ghost that haunts the Ingenium lake seeking revenge—"

"What?" Mackenzie blurted. "You never said anything about. . ."

"We were sort of trying to not die," I said. "I'm telling you now."

"Why did you tell them about the legend?" Toby punched his brother.

"Katrina's article," Taylor said and rubbed his sore arm. "It sounded like that legend. The dead girl was covered in our school colours."

"Former school," Toby added.

"Before Blake passed out, he said the word *revenge*," I told them.

"Oooooo, spooky," Toby said.

"Could the legend be real?" I asked. "Were Lucinda, Alexia, Blake or Katrina mixed up in it?"

"Wait," Toby said, "are you serious?"

I nodded.

"You think that this is payback for a girl who drowned five years ago at Ingenium?" Toby asked.

"What do you know about it?" I asked, and we instinctively huddled closer together.

"I asked my dad about it once," Toby said. "He told me that two girls were taken out at night, covered in paint and then dumped in the school lake as a harmless prank, but one of the girls didn't know how to swim."

None of us knew what to say for a long time. A prank had gone horribly wrong. I wondered if we were all thinking about the stupid pranks we'd pulled. What if something had gone wrong and someone had got hurt? "It was an accident, right?" I said.

The boys shrugged.

"Who would want to seek revenge for the drowned girl?" Mackenzie asked.

"This might have happened about the time that Alexia, Blake and Katrina were at school," Taylor said.

"Yeah, and Lucinda would have been headmistress then," Toby added.

"And covered it up," Mackenzie finished our theory.

Well, almost... "Lucinda would definitely have covered it up if her granddaughter was responsible for someone dying."

"So I can see why Alexia and Lucinda would be targeted but what about Blake and Katrina?" Mackenzie asked.

Then it all snapped into place. "What if Katrina was the other girl in the lake?"

"So she was going to make the people responsible for her friend's death pay?" Mackenzie added.

"Yeah, and then she was going to write a story and tell the world," Toby said. "We've solved it!"

We high-fived each other, but it didn't quite feel right to be celebrating when we found out about something so tragic. One terrible, horrible accident had led to Lucinda's death and a lot of other near-deaths.

"Doesn't Katrina see that she's no better than Lucinda and Alexia?" I said.

"Worse," Toby said. "The girl in the lake was an accident. Katrina killed Mrs Sterling in cold blood."

"I don't know what I'd do if someone hurt my brother," Taylor admitted.

We nodded, even though we must have realized how wrong revenge was. What would I do if someone hurt my dad or grandma or Mackenzie?

"This has to stop and it has to stop now," I said. "You guys go tell your father everything and gather everyone in the lobby. We are going to form a search and rescue party. We know who the murderer is. If we stick together we should be able to find her, right?"

"We should tell Shauna," Mackenzie said. "Have you seen her?"

Toby and Taylor looked at each other as if they were collectively trying to remember.

"She was heading out in her snow gear as Dad was hauling us in here," Taylor added. "She said something to Dad about the ice hotel."

"You round up everyone else," I said, "and we'll find Shauna." I grabbed Mackenzie's hand and led her outside. I punched open the lodge's front door.

"There!" Mackenzie pointed to the faint impression of footprints in the snow ahead, leading directly to the ice hotel. "Maybe those belong to Shauna."

Or Katrina, I thought but didn't say. We followed the trail.

I burst into the ice hotel lobby, calling for Shauna.

A figure shifted from behind Sven's sculpture of Cupid.

I stopped dead in my snowy tracks. Mackenzie ploughed right into me.

"What the. . ." she started but her voice trailed away.

"Stay back!" It was Katrina.

I raised my hands in surrender. How could I continue to be so stupid? We survived her attack in the maze and lost her in the forest only to deliver ourselves like room service to the killer.

"Katrina, we know everything," I blurted. "We understand —"

"Do you?" she shrieked and broke off Cupid's

arrow, pointing the sharp edge right at my chest. "I doubt that. You set me up."

She was talking crazy talk. She stepped closer. "You lured me here. . ." She flicked the arrow in a criss-crossing pattern in front of her like she was Zorro.

I swept Mackenzie behind me. Her body trembled against my back. We both didn't need to die here. I pivoted and shoved Mackenzie towards the door. "Run!"

I whipped around to face Katrina. Death by Cupid's icy arrow. I didn't know whether to laugh or cry. What a stupid – and very Chase – way to die.

21

I crashed to the floor as Mackenzie slammed me from behind and collapsed on top of me.

"What are you doing?" I shouted at her as we scrambled to our feet.

Mackenzie didn't need to say a word. The tables had turned. Shauna had the icy arrow to Katrina's throat.

I hugged Mackenzie. We were saved! Shauna to the rescue like in some old-time Western. *Yeehaw*! I wasn't going to be skewered by Cupid's arrow like the worst Valentine's Day shish kebab ever.

"Thanks, Shauna," I said and raised my hand for a high-five from my new hero. But she left me hanging.

A small stream of blood was dribbling down Katrina's neck where the ice arrow was digging into her skin. Yeah, I knew she was a killer but . . . "Hey, Shauna, let's take Katrina to the lodge. The boys are rounding up everyone. You've caught the killer."

As soon as I said it, I understood that I was dead wrong. The scene in front of me shifted. It was like one of those trick pictures where you see different things based on how you looked at it. I had been so focused on Katrina that I didn't see the other picture. I finally saw Shauna – not the super-perky event-planner that she wanted me to see. I finally saw the scary woman she'd been hiding all along. In a split second, she'd switched from superhero to evil mastermind.

"You killed Lucinda," I said and wished for the millionth time that I could switch off the blurt mechanism that always got me in trouble. Not every thought that popped into my head should fly out of my mouth – and this one could get us killed. Shauna smiled this weird wild smile.

"Why?" Mackenzie asked, shocked by this hairpin turn of events. "You orchestrated this entire weekend. You invited these people here. You misdirected us every chance you got."

When she said it like that, how did we not realize it before now? Shauna had become our friend. She was always there working behind the scenes. Mackenzie grabbed the back of my snowsuit and tugged me out of Shauna's reach.

"Leave!" Shauna screamed at us, spittle flying from her mouth.

"We can't do that," I said. "We can't let you kill anyone else."

"You may have saved Alexia and Blake, but you're not going to save Katrina!" Shauna shouted. "She's going to get what she deserves."

"Please help me," Katrina begged between sobs. "She's Serena Coleman."

"Shut up!" Shauna smacked Katrina to the

ground and held her down with her boot. In the weeks we'd spent with her, I'd never ever seen a hint of the anger that was exploding from Shauna now. How could I have been so blind?

"Serena?" Mackenzie's voice trembled.

"I used to be Serena until they killed me," Shauna said. "I received a scholarship to that horrible school. I thought that it was my chance for a better life." She cackled in this sort of scary way. "Tell them. Tell them what you did to my best friend."

"Parker," I said.

She pointed the arrow at me. "How do you know that name?"

"Katrina wrote a story about a girl named Parker who accidentally drowned," I said.

"Accident!" Shauna laughed again. "Alexia, Blake and Katrina made our lives hell. One night they kidnapped us from our beds, covered us in paint and then launched us into the lake."

"We didn't know Parker couldn't swim," Katrina sobbed. "I'm so sorry. We never meant to hurt anyone."

"You bullied me and Parker all the time," Shauna shouted and pressed her foot deeper into Katrina's chest. Katrina screamed in pain.

I needed to say something to stop her, but Mackenzie thought of something first. "This won't bring Parker back."

"I know, I just don't think that Katrina deserves to keep on living." Shauna grabbed the hood of Katrina's snowsuit and dragged her towards the front door. "Now it's Katrina's turn to take a swim in an icy lake. With any luck, they won't discover her body until spring and by then I'll be long gone."

"Why did you kill Lucinda?" I asked because I needed her to stop moving, and I wanted to know why.

"We were kids," Shauna said. "But she was the adult. She withdrew my scholarship and paid everyone to keep what her granddaughter did a secret. No one believed me. She ruined my life."

"Your life isn't ruined," Mackenzie said.

"Yeah," I agreed. "You are great at what you do. You planned this whole weekend. . ." I stopped when I realized that her life probably was ruined now that she'd killed someone.

"Lucinda wasn't supposed to die like that," Shauna said. "I'd lost twenty-five kilos, dyed my hair and even changed my accent, but Lucinda recognized Serena Coleman. I agreed to meet her at the ice hotel while everyone was watching the Northern Lights. I pushed her. She cracked her head on the unfinished ice bed. I covered her with water. I made up the story about her staying at the cabin. I had Lucinda's phone so I even texted Alexia to buy some time."

"Let Katrina go, and I'm sure we can tell the police about your. . ." What was that phrase that meant she'd done what she'd done because of the bad things that had happened to her?

"Extenuating circumstances," Mackenzie filled in the right words.

"I don't want to hurt you," Shauna said. "I wanted to scare you in the maze. I would never hurt the two of you." Her expression changed from full-on crazy to seriously sad. "You remind me so much of me and Parker. You are two opposites that together make this perfect team. You are very lucky to have each other."

Mackenzie and I looked at each other. We were lucky. I hoped our luck held.

"Forget you ever saw me with Katrina," she said.

"You can't leave me," Katrina begged.

Mackenzie and I held our ground. We weren't going anywhere.

"If you won't do it for me," Shauna said, the cold, scary look was back in her eyes, "then do it for Ariadne."

"What?!" Mackenzie and I said in unison.

"What have you done to my grandma?" I shouted and took a step closer to her. Mackenzie restrained me.

"She figured it out," Shauna said. "Well, not the *why* part, but she knew I was the one who had orchestrate this whole deadly weekend."

"You didn't. . ." I couldn't say the horrible end of that sentence. I hoped Grandma wasn't another accident like Lucinda.

"No, but if you don't find her quickly, she will die." Shauna pulled Katrina kicking and screaming past us. "You've got a choice to make. Try to stop me and your grandma dies because I will never tell you where she is. Or let me walk out that door and I'll tell you everything."

What else could we do? I raised my hands in surrender. I had no intention of letting Shauna hurt Katrina, but we had to play along.

"Chase!" Mackenzie said and stared at me wide-eyed. "We can't stand by and let Shauna kill Katrina."

Shauna pushed open the door. While she was distracted, I winked at Mackenzie. "I have to save my grandma."

We followed Shauna out into the snow. Mackenzie's hands were also held high in surrender. Shauna threw the ice arrow aside and reached into the pocket of her snowsuit. "Ariadne's in the Northern Lights cabin. I tied her up and built a fire, but that was hours ago. If that fire goes out. . ." Shauna tossed a set of keys in a nearby snow pile.

"If that fire goes out. . ." I lunged at Shauna, but Mackenzie tightened her grip. A sob caught in my throat. My sixty-nine-year-old grandma wouldn't survive long in an ice-cold cabin.

"Duck," Mackenzie whispered in my ear and yanked me to the ground.

Snowballs whizzed by from every direction, pelting Shauna again and again until she was beaten to the ground.

It took me a moment to see through the blur of snow that a semi-circle of Winter Wonder Resort guests and staff surrounded us.

I dived for the keys while Mackenzie rushed to the now staggering Katrina, who collapsed in Mackenzie's arms.

I pulled off my gloves and dug through the snow like some crazed mole. My stiffened, nearly frozen fingers finally closed around the keys. I rammed the keys and my hands deep into my snowsuit pockets.

"We thought you might need a little back-up," Toby said as he raced over to me. "We heard

Shauna's crazy talk and the only weapon we had was the snow – and lots of pensioners! Taylor and I always keep a stash of snowballs ready, we just didn't know we'd use them to catch a killer."

I hugged Toby. "Thanks." I couldn't waste any more time. "Send help to the Northern Lights cabin." I tore off towards the line of snowmobiles.

I hopped on the closest one, strapped on a helmet and goggles and revved the engine.

"You aren't going without me!" Mackenzie shouted, snatching up a helmet and goggles. She flung herself on the back of my vehicle. I pointed the snowmobile in the direction of the cabin.

As we sped away, I hoped we weren't too late to save Grandma. Being my grandma was dangerous; I prayed it wasn't deadly.

22

The white landscape turned dull and grey in the setting sun. The world shifted to a scene from a black-and-white movie. A slim finger of smoke guided me forward. It had to be from the fire in the Northern Lights cabin, the only thing keeping my grandma from freezing to death. I pushed the snowmobile to its limits. The elements worked against me. The gusts of wind ripped at my snowsuit and battered the snowmobile. My arms ached from staying my course. Snow peppered my goggles, and at times, the scene ahead was dot to dot – and wiping the spray made it worse. I was terrified by the icy obstacles thrown up at us at top speed, but I was in control. All Mackenzie could do was hang on.

I could see the cabin through the trees. I remembered how Mackenzie and I had danced on that roof. It seemed light years ago.

I gasped as the smoke dwindled into puffs. How long did I have until Grandma froze to death? My cheeks burnt from the cold. My fingers and toes were numb even though they were tucked in the Winter Wonder Resorts thermal gear.

When we reached the cabin, I skidded to a stop. Mackenzie and I were off the snowmobile before it stopped moving. We lunged for the door. I jerked the keys out of my pocket, and accidentally flung them into a nearby snow drift. I fumbled again and again trying to pick them up with gloved hands. My fingers were tingling with cold and shaking with fear. Mackenzie brushed me aside. She removed her gloves and unlocked the door. I rammed it open like a defensive tackle sacking the quarterback.

Grandma was hunched in a wooden chair that was positioned right in front of the fireplace. She was dressed in her designer red snowsuit, gloves and boots.

"Grandma!" I shouted as I dived to her side. She didn't move. Shauna had tied her wrists to the arms of the chair, and her legs were tied together.

"Grandma," I whispered as fear and sadness gripped my chest.

An icy puff escaped her lips. "Chase?"

A hot flash of relief swept through my body. She was alive. While I untied Grandma, Mackenzie stoked the fire until it was blazing again.

"Shauna," Grandma whispered. "It was Shauna."

"We know," I said.

"She's been captured," Mackenzie said and gently hugged Grandma. "Everyone is OK."

I rushed around the cabin and collected every blanket and towel I could find. The sun had set and the temperature was dropping. I positioned the couch in front of the fire and wrapped us up with

Grandma the centre of a Mackenzie and Chase sandwich. My dad had always told me to use body warmth as well as fire, shelter and clothing. He wasn't going to believe me when I told him about our adventure in the Arctic Circle. I might have to delete a few details – like finding dead bodies buried in the ice, being chased by a killer, nearly falling into the frozen lake. . . Actually there wasn't much about the last few days I could tell him.

We sat in silence, letting the warmth and relief soak in. After a long while, Grandma looped one arm around each of us. "Looks like you two disobeyed me again."

"I think our punishment should be that you have to hang out with us for a long, long time," Mackenzie said.

Grandma squeezed us in reply. I think she realized how close she'd come to not being with us for a minute longer. We filled her in on the rest of the story and waited for help to arrive.

Police sirens and lights changed the pitch black outside the cabin to a disco. We returned to the lodge in time to see Shauna being taken away in handcuffs. She opened her mouth to say something. I wondered if she would apologize for almost killing Grandma. But she didn't utter one syllable. Was she sorry for what she'd done? I wondered if her revenge had made her feel better. Grandma gave Shauna a sad smile. Tears streamed down Shauna's face. It was so cold and the situation so desperately sad I thought her tears might freeze like that for ever.

The police ushered us into the lobby where everyone was gathered. All eyes zoomed in on us. People cleared the way for us to take the prime location on one of the lobby's many couches.

"These guys are the real heroes," Toby told the police officer who was interviewing him. "They are the ones who figured it out and caught Shauna."

"We'll need statements from all of you," the police officer said.

Fear zapped me. No one could know Mackenzie's real story. She was still presumed dead. I could see in Grandma and Mackenzie's eyes they were thinking the same thing.

"How did you get here?" Grandma asked the police officer. "I thought the roads were closed."

"Someone pulled strings with headquarters and you became our first priority," one police officer said.

"And some mystery man had cleared a path from the Winter Wonder Resort to the main road," another officer added. "I'm not sure how he did it."

"She," Mackenzie muttered. We knew who that mystery woman was – Mackenzie's mum. We scanned the lobby. I nudged Mackenzie and nodded to the figure in the silver snowsuit slipping to the back of the crowd.

Mackenzie locked eyes with her mum. *Thanks*, she mouthed and gave a sneaky wave as Marilyn slipped out of a side door and out of her daughter's life . . . for now.

"You girls go to your room," Grandma told us with a wink. "I'll talk to the police." She was going to have to cover up our involvement again. We'd have to be erased from any official reports or media coverage.

For once, I didn't mind being sent to my room. We were exhausted but buzzing. It was as if the excitement from the day had electrified my blood. Mackenzie flicked on her computer. I plugged in my phone. Normal everyday things felt strange after everything that had happened.

My phone bleeped with a message. That's when I remembered the email I'd sent to my mom. It couldn't be from her, but I checked anyway.

With a strange mix of excitement and dread, I looked at my messages. How could I be experiencing so many opposite emotions? If it wasn't her, I'd be relieved and disappointed. If it was her, I would be happy and scared. Would she tell me to leave her alone? Did she want anything to do with me? And what if she said she missed me? How would that feel? I didn't miss her. How could I? I'd never met her.

I tapped the unopened message.

Charlotte,

I was overwhelmed to receive your message.

My own mom didn't know that I hated being called Charlotte. She was overwhelmed. That could be good or bad.

I hope this is only the beginning of our correspondence. I want to know absolutely everything about you. Please write back as soon as you can.

I hated that tears were welling in my eyes. I didn't want those few words to mean so much, but they did. Maybe I could have some sort of relationship with my mom after all.

But her message ended with the strangest line. . .

See you soon! Love, Mum

What did that mean? I couldn't travel to England until it was safe for Mackenzie, and Mom wasn't getting released from prison any time soon.

A knock on the door made me jump.

"It's Ariadne," she called through the door.

I shut off my phone. Grandma definitely wouldn't like that my mom had emailed me. Grandma already had enough to deal with. I'd keep my correspondence with Mom a secret for now.

Grandma, Mackenzie and I piled into one bed.

"I've handled everything with the police. Your names will be kept out of it." She was hugging us again. "What would I do without the two of you?"

"You'd be a human icicle by now," I blurted and immediately wished I hadn't.

Mackenzie and Grandma burst out laughing. I couldn't help but join in. We had survived and it was ridiculous and crazy and for some reason really, really funny.

"I think you girls deserve a holiday," Grandma said after our laughter had died down to giggles and then sighs and then a weird silence.

Mackenzie and I groaned. "I'm not sure we can survive another holiday," Mackenzie said.

"Where's your spirit of adventure?" she asked but I could tell exhaustion was kicking in. I was a million years younger, and I was getting more and more tired by the minute. Only now could I feel the hundreds of bumps, scrapes and bruises I'd sustained over the last twenty-four hours.

"I've got it," she said with a yawn after a long while. Our eyes were drooping with sleep. "We'll go to Kuriosity Kingdom."

"In Florida?" Mackenzie asked. "I've never been to the United States."

After all the weird things that had happened in the Maldives and the Arctic Circle, I was ready to go somewhere that spoke my language and where I knew how the world worked. "I've never been to Kuriosity Kingdom," I said. Dad thought amusement parks were silly. He had enough action and adventure in real life when he was in the navy. On vacation he wanted rest and relaxation.

"It's the most sparkly and magical place on the planet," Grandma said her eyes closed in sleep. "What could possibly go wrong there?" she murmured and then began to softly snore.

Mackenzie and I smiled. We were thinking the same thing. Danger followed us everywhere we went. But we would survive no matter what the world threw at us as long as we were together.

TURN THE PAGE TO READ THE WINNING ENTRY FROM THE BROXBOURNE SCHOOL – PATRON OF READING CREATIVE WRITING COMPETITION

AND THE WINNER IS...

Sara Grant serves as the Patron of Reading at The Broxbourne School in Hertfordshire. A Patron of Reading (www.patronofreading.co.uk) is an author, poet, illustrator or storyteller with whom a school forms a long-term attachment. Sara works closely with the school and its dedicated, creative and enthusiastic librarians to promote reading for pleasure and create a genuine reading culture in the school.

As part of her role, in the spring of 2016 she launched the school's first creative writing competition. Nearly one hundred and fifty students participated. The students were asked to write a 500-word mystery inspired by Sara's Chasing Danger series.

The competition was steep with murder and mayhem from around the globe, but Jessica Webster's exciting tale, titled "The Saboteur", won by a nose! She created a satisfying mystery with twists, turns and surprises – and that's not easy to do in a 500-word short story.

Congratulations, Jessica!

THE SABOTEUR

BY JESSICA WEBSTER

"Come on boy," I whispered, hugging my flea-bitten grey Connemara Neo's intricately plaited white mane. If we cleared this jump we'd be through to the final round of the Broxbourne County Horses Trials. A surge of excitement and fear sent shivers down my spine.

Cantering towards the jump, I held my breath as we sailed effortlessly over and landed perfectly. Cheers broke out from the stands as we trotted over to join my friends.

"Well done, Piper!" Lilly exclaimed as Eva and

Poppy beamed at me. "It's just us and Alison in the junior's competition now that Stan's out." We glanced at Alison, smirking at us from atop her Arabian horse, Guldennagel. Whatever happened, we couldn't let her win today.

"Where's my saddle?!" the shout pierced the peaceful silence of the afternoon as we prepared our horses for the cross-country race one hour later. Eva came running out of her cob, Beryl's, stall.

"What's going on?" the competition's judge asked, appearing from round the corner.

"Someone's stolen my saddle!" Eva replied. "So I can't compete!"

Just then, Poppy, usually calm and laid back, came sprinting towards us. "Butterscotch's girth is missing! Someone must have taken it!"

"Right, you two," the judge broke in. "Before you go round accusing anyone, we have to be sure this was deliberate. Could they maybe have just gone missing?"

"No!" they declared in unison. "We're really

careful about our equipment! Now we can't compete in the final round!"

"I'm afraid that's right," the judge agreed, checking the time. "We have to begin the final round soon. We'll look for your equipment and as soon as the competition's finished we will find the culprit."

Directing worried looks at each other, Lilly and I went to fetch our horses while Alison stood by looking smug, as usual.

First up, Alison rode to the starting line, and the second the judge called "Go!" Alison dug her heels into Guldennagel's gleaming sides, and they shot into a gallop down the hill. However, they hadn't gone long when Alison began to slip. We all watched in horror as she tumbled to the ground and lay there. Letting out a small scream, the judge and the rest of us dashed over to her. As she got up and dusted herself off, Alison noticed her audience and suddenly seemed to be in agony."My arm!" she cried. "It's broken!"

The judge examined her and shook her head.

"It's just a bruise, Alison. But what happened?"

"My stirrup leather gave way," Alison shrieked, "but it was brand new!"

As Stan led a spooked Guldennagel over to us, he affirmed, "This was no accident. The stirrup leather's been cut."

We sat in silence in the club office as the judge regarded us sternly, before announcing, "The competition is cancelled until further notice. However I suggest the culprit come forward now before your punishment gets a lot worse."

Nobody moved for what seemed like a decade. The judge sighed and said, "Very well. Every stall will be searched."

After searching fruitlessly for half an hour we arrived at my stall, which Alison seemed particularly excited about. We searched every inch, but to no avail. But then...

"YES! It's a Stanley knife! Piper could have cut my stirrup leathers with this!"

Everyone stared at me in disbelief as the judge

spluttered, "Is this true, Piper?"

"No!" I protested. "I was with Lilly all lunchtime!"

"It's true!" Lilly agreed. "We didn't go anywhere near the tack room!"

Then Stan muttered, "Alison did though."

We all froze as he continued. "I saw her sneak off while we were all having lunch, and she didn't come back for at least twenty minutes."

The judge glared at Alison. "What? No! It wasn't me!" Alison blustered.

"Alison, you were the only one with the opportunity, and we have an eyewitness," the judge stated. "It must have been you. You're banned from the competition."

After a hurried preparation, Lilly and I both ran record times, and ended up tying for first place. As I stood on the podium with her, smiling at everyone cheering ecstatically, I felt happier than I ever had before.

JESSICA WEBSTER

My name is Jessica Webster and I'm 14 years old and in Year 9. I love riding horses at my riding stables, Northaw Riding School, and some of the characters in this story are based on real people at Northaw, including some of the horses! I love creative writing and I hope to do lots more in the future!

Special thanks to everyone at Northaw Riding School, who are the inspiration for this story. Also thanks to my English teacher, Mr Lloyd, who has helped me a lot with my writing this year, and to my family who are all really supportive in everything I do.

ABOUT THE BROXBOURNE SCHOOL

At The Broxbourne School we aim to provide "Achievement and Opportunity for All". Teaching and learning is exemplary and our well-qualified and experienced staff work hard to achieve academic excellence and to engage all students in their studies. We believe that reading for pleasure plays an important part in our success and we work hard throughout the school and in partnership with parents to encourage and promote wider reading. The life of the school is enriched by an exceptional programme of opportunities outside the classroom and we are delighted that Sara Grant, as our Patron of Reading, has added a new and exciting dimension to these. In particular, her author talks and creative writing competition have inspired many pupils and we are thrilled that she has arranged for the winner to be honoured in this book.

Paula Humphries, Headteacher

DON'T MISS...